Infinite
Blue

Infinite Blue

DARREN GROTH
& SIMON GROTH

ORCA BOOK PUBLISHERS

Library and Archives Canada Cataloguing in Publication

Groth, Darren, 1969-, author
Infinite blue / Darren Groth & Simon Groth.

Issued in print and electronic formats.
ISBN 978-1-4598-1513-1 (softcover).—ISBN 978-1-4598-1514-8 (PDF).—
ISBN 978-1-4598-1515-5 (EPUB)

I. Groth, Simon, author II. Title.
PS8613.R698I54 2018   jc813'.6   c2017-907947-6
c2017-907948-4

Library of Congress Control Number: 2018933711

Summary: In this novel for teens, an elite swimmer and a talented artist
face a life-altering incident that tests the limits of their love.

*Orca Book Publishers is dedicated to preserving the environment and has
printed this book on Forest Stewardship Council® certified paper.*

Orca Book Publishers gratefully acknowledges the support for its publishing
programs provided by the following agencies: the Government of Canada through
the Canada Book Fund and the Canada Council for the Arts, and the Province of British
Columbia through the BC Arts Council and the Book Publishing Tax Credit.

Edited by Sarah N. Harvey
Cover artwork by Iveta Karpathyova
Design by Teresa Bubela
Darren Groth photo by Lauren White

ORCA BOOK PUBLISHERS
orcabook.com

Printed and bound in Canada.

21 20 19 18 • 4 3 2 1

Rip

Clayton Sandalford put his head down, kicked his legs, clawed at the ocean with everything he had.

A count to five.

To ten.

Another ten, fueled by a gurgled scream.

He lifted his head up from the surging current, paddling limply. Nothing gained. In fact, he was even farther away. The retreating beach was blurred, pixelating through the salt water in his eyes.

This shouldn't have happened. He'd been swimming between the flags, watching the breakers, noting the subtle shift from green to blue that he wanted to emulate on his sketching app. Clayton Sandalford was no lifeguard, but he knew his water safety. He'd adjusted with the sweep, dived beneath the bigger waves. He'd done nothing wrong. In the end, pure intent and blameless action hadn't mattered. The water had flexed one of its billion muscles and Clayton, powerless against the Pacific, had been pulled out to a place of no return. During seventeen short years, he'd learned to swim and learned to survive, but doing both at the same time was too much to ask.

The rip continued to drive Clayton toward the horizon. Slowing his leaden legs and shoulders, he let his head fall back and closed his eyes. Not long now. Soon the water would shift its irresistible force from along the surface to down into the depths. It would tug at him, coaxing him to take a last breath and surrender. He was tempted not to argue.

I'm sorry, Mummu.

No!

Clayton slapped once more at the water, kicked harder.

"Whoa, whoa! Stop flailing, hey?"

Clayton opened his eyes and brought his head forward. The sight of another human being ten feet away had him scrambling to get closer.

"Dude, seriously, stop! Chill. Stay calm. Breathe. The worst of the rip's just about done."

As though on command, the churning current released him. Clayton was back in calm, bobbing waves.

"We're going to have to swim around the point to get back to shore. It's a bit of a hike. Think you can make it?"

"I don't know." Clayton's voice sounded foreign to his own ears, choked and afraid.

"You know what? It's easy. Keep rolling your arms over. Kick every few strokes. There's no rush. Take as much time as you need. If you get tired we can stop. Float on your back for a bit. Move your hands back and forth to help your buoyancy. Whatever it takes. We'll make it back. I'll stay with you. Right alongside."

"Who are you?" he said.

"I'm Ash."

"You're not a lifeguard?"

"No."

"Where the hell did you come from?"

"Look, I can play twenty questions out here, but I don't think you can. And you don't want the water asking another one."

Ash moved in beside Clayton. As instructed, Clayton began rolling his arms over. Inexplicably, he felt strong, light. The forces he'd almost surrendered to now seemed to be at his mercy.

He crawled out of the surf, coughing and rasping through a tight chest. He touched the sand with cramping, slightly swollen hands. His feet tingled. Everything else ached. He collapsed and rolled onto his back, staring at the sky.

A girl saved me, he thought. A selfless stranger. A hero. Like those dolphins of sea-rescue folklore, she'd appeared out of nowhere—more vision than substance—easing his panic and patiently guiding his long journey back to shore.

There was something else about her too. Something certain. The way she knew what to say and when to say it. The feeling of security he'd felt swimming beside her. On the verge of allowing the sea to take him down, Clayton had doubted he could choose his destiny. Perhaps destiny had chosen him instead?

Ash.

Clayton propped himself on his elbows in time to watch her emerge from the shallows, lifting her knees high and shaking the water from her hair, as if she'd been frolicking in the breakers rather than rescuing a drowning boy. She smiled and jogged up, showing no sign of breathlessness. Clayton dropped back to the sand, and she stood over him.

"You okay?" she said.

He nodded.

"Sure?"

A second nod.

"Can you speak?"

"Yes," he wheezed. "Thank you. For saving me."

"I only helped. You saved yourself." Ash adjusted her position, blocking out a sliver of sunlight behind her. "You're a bit burnt." She looked him up and down. "Not bad." She grinned. "The burn, I mean—not the body. I mean, the body's fine. Nice, actually." She shook her head as though internally chiding herself.

"Um." Clayton blinked at her. "Okay." Squinting, he took in her shape silhouetted against the glare. Athletic upper body tapering to a slim waist and long, muscular legs. But his eyes were drawn to her shoulders, broad and powerful in a way that reminded him of a classical statue.

He sat up and examined his red, raw hands. Ash scanned the beach, then sat beside him. They watched the water, the rhythmic curl of the waves showing no sign of undercurrent.

"You said you weren't a lifeguard."

"I'm not."

"You look like one. I mean, you look like you could go out and do that again without breaking a sweat. Are you an athlete?"

Ash smiled. Clayton liked how broad it was, how it rivaled her shoulders. It wriggled into his tight chest, opening it, filling it with a tiny, warming sun. They were the only two people on the beach. He studied her face. Beneath her tanned cheeks she may have been blushing. It was hard to tell.

"I swim a bit."

"More than a bit, I'm guessing."

"ASHLEY RAY DRUMMOND!"

The pair turned toward the urgent voice. A block-like woman in a tracksuit had made her way through the nearby boulders and was charging in their direction. Her right arm was bound in a sling, pinned against her chest.

"Oh boy," said Ash.

"You know her?"

"More than a bit."

Ash stood and waved. Clayton attempted to stand with her, but his legs wobbled and he sat down again. He folded his arms and tried not to look like a near-drowning victim.

The block-woman stomped up to them. "What the hell are you doing way over here?"

"Hi, Mum."

"Don't bloody *hi* me! You do realize how much this little diversion screws up your training plan, don't you?"

Ash glanced down at Clayton. He smiled weakly.

"Something came up. Something important," she said, turning back to her mother and shading her eyes. "A matter of life and death."

"Life and death?"

"Yes, Mum. Life and death. This is…" She paused— he hadn't told her his name. "He was caught in a rip."

Blythe Drummond grunted, then aimed the full fire of her gaze at Clayton, burning him from head to toe. After ten full seconds of silence, she said, "You were rescued by someone who'll be remembered forever. You're a very lucky boy." She stretched the fingers peeking from the cuff of the sling. "Ashley Ray, the personal trainer is waiting for you back there." She turned on her heel without another look at either Clayton or her daughter. "I'm paying her two hundred bucks an hour, which means you have two minutes to get your backside over to the main beach again."

Blythe Drummond was well out of sight before Clayton realized he had been clenching his teeth. "I guess you've got to go," he said.

"Yeah." Ash squatted down and looked again out to the waves. "Think I might swim back."

"Won't that take longer than two minutes?"

"Yeah." She smiled again, stoking the tiny sun in Clayton's chest. "It will."

They watched a perfect barrel wave roll over the break.

"Well…" She brushed sand off her hand and held it out to him. "See ya."

He took her outstretched hand and shook it slowly, prolonging the physical contact for as long as possible. She didn't seem to mind.

"Do you come here often?" He cringed. The awful cliché had tumbled out before he could stop it. "I mean, you know, the training thing. Is that something you do a lot? Here?"

Ash stood tall and took a step toward the water. "Training is pretty consistent. Pretty sure I'll be here tomorrow. About the same time." She scooped up a handful of water and splashed it on her chest. "I still don't know your name."

"It's Clayton. Clay."

"Maybe I'll see you tomorrow then, Clay."

"Maybe."

"And seriously, stay out of the rips, okay?"

"I will."

Ash smiled, nodded. Then she swam away.

Clayton lay flat on the sand. Unlike Ash, he would walk along the beach back to the patrolled area. But not yet.

He studied the hand that had held hers. The skin felt hot. It was as if all the blood in his body had gathered in his prickling fingers.

Infinite

One

Clayton hustled along the hallway between the locker rooms and the marshaling area, trying to look like he belonged. He frowned at his tablet and muttered words of coachspeak he'd picked up over the past year. He hoped no one would realize the accreditation hanging from his lanyard was a fake, an oldie from one of Ash's past meets. It seemed unlikely. Everyone in the hallway had tunnel vision. Long trains of Lycra swimsuits and polyester tracksuits shunted back and forth as events were called out over the PA. Mostly he kept out of the way, avoiding the churn. At the end of the hallway he found the secluded room he was searching for and opened the door.

Relief flushed through him—no one else was there. The meeting had been his idea, but the place was her suggestion: a nondenominational chapel tucked away in the deeper recesses of the complex. Though the chapel was purpose-built for athletes seeking a little divine advantage, the walls were covered with abstract art rather than religious imagery. A stand containing a dish of holy water stood sentry beside the rear pews.

"We can't make out here—Dad would have a fit," said Ash, emerging from a small alcove near the altar. "And not right before a race." She wore a robe over her swimsuit. In her right hand she carried her cap and goggles. Her tone was fake admonition, and she spoke through the smile that never failed to floor Clayton.

"I just wanted to wish you luck," he replied.

"Yeah, sure. You could have done that with a text, you know."

"Wouldn't have been the same."

She smiled again. "No, it wouldn't have."

They kissed. Clayton sensed the coiled tension within Ash and pressed against her. He loved that she still got nervous before a race she couldn't lose.

"I've got something for you," he said, pulling away and digging in his pocket. After a few seconds he extracted a small box.

She arched an eyebrow. "Um, aren't you supposed to get down on one knee?"

"Not right before a race."

She laughed, her fingers fumbling as she flipped the lid open. The ring was a plain silver band etched with a Celtic design. She ran a finger over its surface.

"It's beautiful. What's the little figure?"

"It's a water lover. From Scottish mythology."

"Water lover?"

"Yeah. They're nocturnal creatures who live underwater and are completely translucent. The story goes that water lovers are usually mistaken for ghosts, so people are afraid of them. But it's actually the water lovers who are more scared of humans. The thing they fear most is being caught and exposed to the sunlight and air. When that happens a water lover instantly melts. She falls through your fingers and forms a puddle on the floor."

"Since when do you know anything about Scottish mythology?"

"Since the shop assistant told me."

Ash took the ring from the box and slipped it over her right ring finger. It was much too large, and she wiggled it.

"Oh crap," said Clayton. "I'm sorry."

She laughed and transferred it to her thumb. "I love it. I'm going to wear it for this race."

"Isn't that a no-no?"

"I don't care." She turned her hand over, admiring the glint of the ring off the soft light of the chapel's electric candles. "Don't let me fall through your fingers, hey?"

Clayton kissed her hand. "I won't."

"I love you, Clay."

"I love you too, Ash."

They held each other again. In the nearby stand, the holy water shimmered in its shallow marble bowl.

Two

Clayton sat in the stands alone.

But not by himself. The stadium brimmed with faces all too familiar, characters all too easy to parody. Fathers wearing monogrammed polo shirts and thumbing stopwatches. Painted mothers with peroxide hair. Little brothers and sisters waving signs and pom-poms and ice-cream sandwiches that leaked over their hands. Among them Clayton was a foreigner. A dark smudge on their fluorescent sports logos. That was how he liked it. He enjoyed the atmosphere and the crowd, but he didn't cheer. And the people who banged on the seats—they were hilarious.

Tablet and stylus in hand, he drew the chaos around him, distilling it into pixels, panels, speech bubbles. He'd finished an outline for a new character—a dancing cockroach with a pom-pom on the end of each antenna—when he felt the weight of being watched. He looked up. The woman in the next seat was giving him the once-over. His mind's eye immediately caricatured her.

Look at the smoker's upper lip, a wrinkled duck bill.

Too much mascara makes her eyes sink back into her skull.

Let's call her Shaz.

The disdain in the woman's gaze was barely masked. He twirled his stylus and offered a wry smile. Shaz nodded. She began to chew, though there didn't seem to be anything in her mouth.

"Morning," said Clayton.

"You takin' splits there, love?"

"I'm sorry?"

"You takin' splits? I'd like to see 'em at the end if you are."

Splits were lap times, or maybe lap ratings, something like that. Without Ash in his life, he might have suggested the woman take her strange fetish next door to the gymnastics arena.

"No, I'm drawing."

"Oh, are you, like, an event artist? You know, pictures of the pool and the kids!" The woman clapped her hands. "I'd love a picture of my Sally. She's competing in the race coming up—the eight-hundred. Got a chance at a medal, she has. Not gold. No. Bronze, I reckon.

Maybe silver if she does a major PB. Yeah, we could get on the dais for sure. The eight-hundred—it's Sal's best one."

Ash's best too, thought Clayton. She'd won the two-hundred and four-hundred events by wide margins, but the eight-hundred-meter was her pet. "She's the prototypical specimen for the eight," Coach Dwyer liked to say. "I only wish they had longer distances for the girls." Clayton couldn't speak to the truth of the "prototypical specimen" claim, but he knew Ash was something special. Long bones bound by carved muscles and leather tendons. Hands like ceiling-fan blades. And, of course, those shoulders, wide as a tank. Anatomically she was built to scythe the water like so many of her competitors. What set Ash apart, though, was her grace. She was an artist, at one with her medium. Sometimes, Clayton swore, you couldn't tell where she stopped and the water started.

Vanishing act aside, it didn't prevent the pain Ash endured. *The eight hurts like hell,* she confided to Clayton once. *The best way to do it is flat out. Right from the starter's pistol, you sprint.* She said it without the slightest hint of dread. In fact, her tone was not far short of *bring it on.* Clayton suspected it was because she could disappear for eight-plus minutes.

"The eight-hundred?" a second voice chimed in from the seats behind. "You've seen Ash Drummond, right?"

Clayton took stock of the eavesdropper—another pair of lash-blast eyes atop a long nose that hooked at the end. *Kaz.* He searched for a smirk, an arched eyebrow, anything to indicate that this person knew exactly who Clayton was and why he was there. Nothing. Just open inquiry and mascara. He glanced down at his screen, wondering if maybe he had accidentally shown one of his "Ash sketches," the absent-minded doodles he made on the side between his proper cartoons. The tablet was asleep.

Shaz recrossed her legs and gave a small shake of her head. "That girl is something, I tell ya. The next big thing. Got Olympic gold in her future and everything that goes along with it."

"Yeah, I reckon," said Kaz, nodding thoughtfully.

"Don't get me wrong, I love my Sal. Love her and her sisters with all my heart. She makes me so proud every time she races. Great little swimmer, she is. And the national team…it's not impossible. One day, maybe. But, as good as she is, Sal is never going to give Ash Drummond a run for her money. No. That girl is untouchable."

A wave of noise broke over the grandstand. The contest below was nearing its finish. Two boys—one in a blue cap, the other in a white cap—had separated from the field and were flailing for the final touch.

The water bulged with the strain of their lithe frames, their desperation for a fingernail's advantage in the dying meters. The lunge came, and they sprang out of the wash that followed them to the wall. The crowd commotion dipped for a second, breath held for the result. The electronic scoreboard showed nothing, delaying, teasing. Then, with a click of some unseen magician's fingers, the result flashed up. A pocket of supporters in the eastern stand jumped out of their seats and shouted. The white-cap boy raised and waggled a single finger in a cocky "number one" gesture. The blue-cap kid slumped over the lane rope. Tiny waves enveloped him and lapped gently against his crimson cheeks.

"I've seen the ones who can't cope with success," said Kaz. She spoke louder to be heard over her own raucous applause. "It's always the same. They get a bit of the spotlight, and they can't handle it. Sponsorship deals come along. The media comes calling. They start thinking they're a bit too special. Fame is a lot more fun than following a black line for hours on end. They go to parties, get in the social scene. And not once do they look behind them. They don't see what it did for the previous 'star.' They think they can be different." Kaz adjusted her charm bracelet and nodded. "That Ash Drummond though? Yeah, something is different about that kid."

"She certainly comes across as a lovely young girl." Shaz put her hands in her lap and turned back over her shoulder. "Really seems to have her head screwed on. Of course, you can never really know what goes on behind the scenes, right?"

Clayton stifled a laugh and pressed the power button on his tablet. He stared at the rough sketch on screen, the dozen lines that would soon find form. An offer to draw the Shaz's Sal was out of the question, but he wanted to offer her some small gift of goodwill.

"I hope your daughter has a good swim today," he said. "Maybe she'll get the silver."

Shaz smiled and pulled her shoulders back. "Oh, thank you, darl! Thanks very much!"

Contestants for the eight-hundred were filing out of the marshaling area. None of them—not even Ash Drummond—recognized the shimmering breath of Fate accompanying their entrance. For everyone present, this was just another event on the program.

Three

Ash sat in the plastic chair behind lane four, head crammed inside a maroon latex cap, body squeezed into black Lycra. The blood in her temples thumped along with the music blaring from the bud in her left ear. Her feet bounced and danced. Somewhere amid the pounding drums and soaring guitars a grounded thought pushed through.

Feel the water, Ash.

It was the one thought that underscored Coach Dwyer's final instructions (*"Don't go out too hard…Clean turns…Stay in the middle of your lane…Don't let anyone surf off you…"*) and her mother's self-help sound bites (*"You are the best…You cannot be denied…You were made for this journey…This is your moment to own…"*).

She turned off the music, removed the bud from her ear. She leaned forward in her chair and scrunched her eyes, trusting the sparks and blooms and fountains of white behind her eyelids to center her. They didn't. The sound of a wolf whistle—*wanker*—in the crowd jolted her focus. The smell of fries and ketchup ended it completely. She opened her eyes and cricked her neck, side to side. Her feet continued to hop and bop.

A contrasting sight sat at Ash's right elbow. The competitor in lane five was in her zone, and it wasn't a friendly place. Her body was hunched, her face severe and frozen. The fluorescent-orange goggles belied a dangerous gaze. Her jaw was locked in a clench, the muscles in her cheeks like knuckles. She was a simmering cauldron. A building tsunami. Ash leaned over and tapped the side of her chair.

"Hey, Tiff, what sits at the bottom of the sea and shakes?" She waited, allowing the silence between them to hang. "A nervous wreck." She tapped the chair a second time. "Have a good one."

"Piss off," replied Tiff, lifting her chin.

Ash laughed. "You're always so wound up, Tiffany! Chill." She considered recommending a psychologist, then thought better of it. "You got to enjoy it out here. Lose yourself in the water."

"I'll enjoy it," said Tiff, "when I lose *you* in the water."

Ash nodded—fair enough—and leaned back. Tiff Beeksma had been chasing her for three years and had never got within shouting distance. But was that a guarantee of dominance today? The question was barely complete before Blythe's voice crashed her thoughts: *There are no Cinderellas in this world.*

Ash noted her rival's new look—a neck-to-ankle swimsuit that resembled sharkskin and claimed to bite big chunks out of personal bests. Tiff's glass slipper perhaps? Hopefully not. The last thing she wanted was Coach sitting her down, running a hand across his comb-over and insisting Ash also wear a glorified garbage bag. The thought of it made her skin prickle.

The PA trumpeted her name. She followed the response protocol Blythe had designed for these moments—stand up, nod, wave to all sections. Confident but not cocky. Assured but not arrogant. She sat back down and looked over to the front section of the eastern stand where her parents were positioned. Blythe lifted a fist and mouthed the words *winning time.* Her father, Len, settled his full-body nervous tic long enough to bring his hands together in prayer. Ash turned her attention to the western stand and after a few seconds spotted Clayton hunched over his screen.

"Aw, come on, Clay," she said. "You could at least pretend."

She smirked and touched the new ring on her thumb. Clayton wasn't into PDAs and shunned the waving and the screaming and the—God forbid—blowing kisses that the showboating boyfriends specialized in. She liked to give him a hard time about it—*How about a big smooch, huh?*—but in truth she appreciated it. Blythe called him ComiCon, without affection. What Blythe and others failed to see—what Ash saw and marveled at—was that although he seemed oblivious, Clayton could recount, often with alarming clarity, Ash's every stroke. He understood her swims in a way that no one else did. He *felt* it— the luminous water, the burning pain, the worry about every imperfect kick and the correction that inevitably followed. He was there in the lane with her. And though she would never say it out loud, the last thing she wanted to do was disappoint him.

Her heart boomed, and she felt the shudders of his. Together, they could have been mistaken for the continental shrugs of the seafloor.

Ash walked to the pool edge, knelt down and scooped the water. She splashed her shoulders and chest. Thighs and calves. The spaces between her toes. She brought her goggles down to the bridge of her nose and slapped the sides of her swim cap with the butts of her hands. Responding to the marshal's requests, she mounted the block. The starter commanded the field to "take your mark" and Ash obliged. Her feet assumed the position: the left gripped the block's front edge like a bear's claw, the right remained planted toward the back of the platform.

She pulled back and crouched, chin on her chest, body locked and loaded. Her skin was sprayed with goose bumps. The buzzy peal of the starter's signal rang out, and Ash catapulted into the air. The split second between weightlessness and the water's first slap always triggered a succession of unbidden images. On this day, Ash saw three.

1. Herself at ten years old, standing in front of the ancient Leverton pool, gold medal for the fifty free around her neck.
2. Clayton walking her through his creative process, his hands gliding over the screen as he turned pixels into characters and stories.
3. Herself in the break off Cora Heads, bodysurfing with a pod of dolphins.

Then she was in the water's embrace. Timeless instinct and modern muscle memory took over. Her body became a seamless tide as exertion transformed into beauty. The girl who would come to be known as Wake began easing away from her rivals.

One thought pulsed in her mind:

I'm home.

Four

Clayton sat in the stands and drew.

Usually, when the starter siren blared, he would snap his eyes up from the screen and zero in on Ash's lane, leaning forward, hands nervously occupied. On this day, for reasons he couldn't fathom, Clayton did not look up. Instead he opened a fresh canvas and ran the tip of the stylus over the glass, allowing lines and shadings and flourishes to emerge more or less on their own. He saw the piece taking shape, but he wasn't focused. He was adrift. Later he wondered if he knew this day—this art—would be different, if he somehow understood things would never be the same. In the moment, though, his actions were borne of impulse.

Just stay with it, Ash, he thought. Stay cool. Clear your mind and let the timing take over. One day that perfect swim is going to happen. I know it.

Even without watching, Clayton knew well the sounds of a race playing out. Loud cheers. Warm applause. Restrained, almost begrudging acknowledgment—the sort reserved for sure things like Ash Drummond. Today the sounds fell outside the norm. Urgency underlined the crowd commotion. High-pitched squeals pierced the general hum; seat banging and foot stomping paced the action. Clayton felt a trapdoor open in the floor of his stomach. Excitement like this could mean only one thing.

She's getting beaten.

The din broke its banks. Clayton fumbled the stylus. It bounced around his feet. He wiped his mouth with his sleeve, bracing himself for the worst. Finally he looked up. A sea of standing bodies surrounded him, blocking views of the pool, the scoreboard and anything else that would confirm Ash's fall. A Nike-clad family in the neighboring row of seats danced and twittered, their wide eyes and waving hands clear evidence of an upset. Shaz, pinkie fingers planted in the corners of her mouth, released a whistle that sailed through the noise like a harpoon in flight.

Clayton laid his tablet down and stood. He hoped he could catch sight of Ash, make her feel better for a few seconds with a small wave or a pulled face. But once above the crowd, the sand clogging Clayton's heart was swept away. Ash sat on the lane rope, hands clapping above her head. Her easy, generous smile filled the stadium. She was alone. The rest of the field continued to race. Their leader, in lane six, remained half a pool length from the finishing wall. On the giant scoreboard, the phrase *WORLD RECORD* sat conspicuously beside Ash's name and time.

"Is that real?" he whispered to himself. "What does that mean?"

It took another minute and forty-nine seconds for the final competitor to touch home. Ash climbed out of the pool and planted her feet on the deck. Bypassing an entourage of officials and media, she headed toward the roiling crowd, specifically "Team Drum" in the front row of the eastern stand. From the opposite side, Clayton studied each interaction as it took place. Coach Dwyer shaking hands for a good twenty seconds. Len looking to the heavens before hugging his only child, tears streaming.

And Blythe.

She might have been the only person in the arena remaining seated. Ash knelt on one knee before her. The foreheads of mother and daughter touched. They traded a few words. When Ash returned to standing, her diamond smile had dulled, the expression that replaced it somewhere between *What did you expect?* and *What's next?*

Clayton grabbed his tablet, wriggled past the rest of the still-celebrating spectators and ran down the concrete stairs to the front of the stand. He leaned out over the rail as Ash slowly circled the pool deck, the eye of a well-wishing, camera-flashing storm.

Clayton waved and yelled her name.

She couldn't hear.

He shouted again.

Nothing.

The storm drew level, then passed. Clayton stepped back, craning his head left and right to catch a glimpse of her through the throng. But as the circus passed with no acknowledgment, his shoulders slumped. Somewhere in the crush, he'd lost sight of her altogether.

She's out of the water, he thought. She's not supposed to disappear.

~⊙

"Hey, Clay!"

She stood below him, skin glistening, hands planted on her hips, smirk scuttling about the corners of her mouth. She'd pushed through the wall of media to seek him out.

"Come down."

Clayton climbed over the railing and scrambled down the side of the stands to the deck surface to meet her face-to-face. Ash enveloped him in a warm, wet embrace.

"You were incredible," he said.

"Yeah, it felt good in there. I—" She paused and pointed at the tablet. "What are you working on?"

"Seriously? You've just broken a fricking world record!"

"I'm having a good day. I want to know how yours is going."

"Not nearly as good as yours."

"Let me see."

"I'll show you later."

"Come on, Clay."

Clayton looked around at the waiting media throng. They wanted to see too. He woke the screen and flipped it around to show Ash. Just Ash.

"I was mucking around."

She stared. For a brief second Clayton thought she might slap the tablet out of his hands. Ash's eyes widened and her lips parted, releasing a tiny gasp. But then the shock—if that's what it was—faded out.

"Whoa! Are you kidding? That's amazing."

Clayton shrugged, trying to disguise his soaring joy. She's back, he thought. Fully present. She leaned toward him, and they shared a kiss and a second hug.

"You think you're pretty shit-hot, don't you?" he whispered.

"Too hot for you to handle, boy." She laughed. "I've got to go. My public needs me."

∽೨

It was the moment they had all been waiting for. It had been foretold by a good many. Coach Dwyer had bet his house on it and lost his wife in the process. Len had always believed, trusting the Good Lord favored those who constantly gave thanks and praised His name. And, of course, Blythe had dreamed it, visualized it. *Willed* it. Clayton dwelled on this for a minute, feeling an uncomfortable itch settle in the small of his back. Blythe Drummond had been vindicated. Her daughter's entrance upon the world stage was so much more than earned or achieved—it was a square-up. Redemption and revenge all rolled into a neat package.

∽೨

Clayton retreated back to the stands, wondering how long he would have to wait for the medals and conferences and glad-handing to wind down. He checked his social-media feeds and mentions. He "liked" a few posts from friends and followers. Absently he flicked to the picture he'd put together during Ash's race, the image that had been more whim than choice.

Most of the canvas was taken up with rich watercolor textures of deep blues and greens, the hues of a hostile wave of surf caught at its peak, a tsunami set to swamp anything in its path.

In the center was Ash.

Her back was turned to the viewer, and she faced directly into the colossal wave. She wore her racing swimsuit, cut low on her back so she could have more of her body in contact with the water. Arms extended. Feet apart and planted. Her hair was down, a tangle of thin black tentacles mingling with the blue.

Clayton stared, unblinking, for a full minute. He recalled Ash's initial stunned reaction—no wonder, he thought. He closed the canvas and saw that the image had acquired a title, a name automatically assigned by the app: *Source01*.

This wasn't a comic strip. This wasn't a caricature. Nothing he had drawn prior resembled this piece, not in form or theme or execution. So what *was* it? He couldn't say. The only thing he could pinpoint was the unease the work provoked, the small sloshy churn it stirred up in the pit of his stomach.

He thought seriously about hitting the Trash icon. Without Ash's ultimate admiration for the pic, he would've done so in an instant. Instead he put the device to sleep and tried to cast the image from his mind.

Five

After the meet Clayton steered the car out into traffic. Months of badgering had led to Len's allowing Ash to borrow his restored Corvette on a semipermanent basis (not agreed to was his daughter's regularly palming off driving duties to her boyfriend, but Len was none the wiser). As the grumbling engine settled into cruising speed, Clayton stole a glance at Ash in the passenger seat. She was looking at the ring on her thumb, admiring the light reflected off it. The suburban streets, freshly cleansed from a recent downpour, rolled away beneath them.

"That was a busy day, wasn't it?" she said. On cue, her phone, dumped in one of the cupholders, came to life with the sound of a cartoon explosion. It was the fourteenth text she had received since the start of the drive home. She opened the message.

"Okay, so this is some rep named Joe Gauthier, from what I assume is a very large sports management agency."

"Sounds like a fake name," said Clayton.

"Joe wants to express his 'sincere congratulations on establishing a new world mark.' Thanks, Joe. He is also interested in 'setting up a meeting to talk about what we can do for you.'"

"Sure. For *you*."

Ash would not reply to Joe Gauthier—there was no need. Blythe would respond to him and all the other "drones" who were suddenly desperate for Ash's attention and time.

"Joe says I have a nickname now. 'Wake.'"

Clayton scoffed. "Did he make that up?"

"I heard a reporter say it when I was walking through the carpark."

"Ha!" Clayton shook his head. "Whatever." He eased the car into the passing lane and overtook a city bus. "What were you going to tell me, by the way?"

"When?"

"After the swim. You started to say something about feeling good in the pool."

"Oh." She sat up straighter in her seat. "It's nothing."

"Nothing?"

"Yeah."

"I'm not Joe Gauthier. You can tell me."

"It's nothing. *Literally* nothing. Don't worry about it."

Clayton frowned. "You know you're being super weird right now."

Ash shrugged and started flipping through her social-media feed, scrunching her face as she scrolled. On the windshield drops of rain gathered, blurring the road ahead before vanishing under the swipe of the wiper blades.

"Your dad sure was emotional," said Clayton, changing conversational tack.

"You know it. Mum was choked too."

"Yeah right."

"What?"

Clayton raised an eyebrow. "Choked?"

"Yes, choked."

"Did she cry? You know, like, actual tears?"

Ash rolled her eyes and suppressed a smile. "Sick burn, bro."

Blythe's disdain of crying was common knowledge in the Drummond household. She viewed it as indulgent, a waste of energy. *Are your issues resolved by bawling like a baby? Does it find you a new job? Put money in your bank account? Bring back someone who's dead?* Clayton once suggested to Ash that it was all an elaborate ruse to cover for the tragic loss of her tear ducts in a bungled surgery.

Len more than made up the difference. He was prone to welling up over TV ads, Bible passages and everything in between. Blythe wouldn't chastise her husband in these moments of weakness. She would simply stare at him, unblinking, one eyebrow arced on her forehead, her gaze like a concrete dam set down at the mouth of a river.

Clayton often wondered how these two people had ever gotten together and made something as perfect as Ashley Ray Drummond. There was no joy in their two-decades-long union as far as he could see. No warmth or tenderness. Nothing that resembled the depth of devotion he shared with their daughter. To Clayton, it was extraordinary that Len and Blythe could even share the same house.

Ash rolled the window down and stuck her hand out. It dipped and darted in the onrushing wind and rain.

"That drawing you did today," she said. "It was different. What inspired you to do it?"

"I don't know." Clayton shifted in his seat as he turned a corner.

"Did you, like, have a vision or something during the race?"

"You're making fun of me."

"I'm not. I'm being totally serious."

"I was just fooling around. I'm going to delete it."

"Don't do that. Keep it."

"No."

"Please."

"No."

"Please. For now. For me."

A long pause.

"Okay, fiiiine," he said.

Ash nodded and squeezed Clayton's knee.

"So what happens now?" he asked.

"Keep heading on Expressway toward Coro Drive, then hang a right at the overpass onto Hale Street."

"That's not what I meant, smartarse."

"I'm not being a smartarse. We keep doing what we do. We head home. We call each other tonight. We go to the movies tomorrow afternoon. Sit in the back row and make out like we always do. I'm not going to change, Clay. I'm not going to become someone you don't recognize."

Ash wound the window back up and leaned her head against it. She twisted the ring on her thumb.

"This is a big deal," said Clayton. "You can't promise that everything is going to stay the same." He waved at the phone, now back in the cup holder. "The agents and the press and the media managers—it's all nuts."

"You want me to stop it?"

"Of course not! This is once-in-a-lifetime stuff."

"So are we," said Ash.

The heavens opened fully as Clayton cruised into the driveway of his townhouse complex, pulling in close to the front door before cutting the engine. The two of them threw open their doors, leaped out into the downpour and dashed for the small dry refuge beneath the front-door overhang. Ash flicked the water from her face and brow and pulled the hood of her sweatshirt over her head.

"Thanks for driving," she said, raising her voice above the clamor. "Might need to trade the car for a dinghy to get home though."

She offered Clayton a cheesy grin. She stood with her back to the door, brass knocker above her head like mistletoe. A saturated cord of hair clung to her cheek. Clayton gently cleared it away from her face and back over her ear.

"Hey." He cleared his throat. "We're going to be okay." He took her hand and scrutinized it. "Here, look. It says so in your palm. We're going to be with each other forever. We're going to get married, have some kids, live in a fancy house. Oh, look—it's got a pool!"

Ash jerked her hand out of his grasp before the inevitable spit. "Too slow, jerk."

They wrapped their arms around each other and kissed. In the middle of the driveway the storm drain overflowed, sending rivulets scurrying to all points of the compass. One arrived at the overhang and created a thin puddle around their feet.

When Ash drove away—the muffled cartoon explosions of new messages accompanying her departure—Clayton removed the tablet screen from his satchel and opened *Source01*. Tiny flecks of water hit the glass surface, distorting the pixels underneath. He wiped them off with his finger, not realizing the app was set to the smudge tool. The image now contained large blue splotches, as though he'd attacked it with a sponge. The dappled sunlight on the waves was blurred into a blue-green morass. The delicate tendrils of Ash's hair were teased into thick black streaks.

His finger hovered over the button for a second before tapping hard enough to make a hollow knock against the glass. *Source01* disappeared. Ash may have wanted him to keep it, but she'd get over it.

A slow, childish singsong ran through his mind as he went inside, something straight out of a schlocky horror movie:

It's raining, it's pouring,
No more freaky drawing.

Six

Clayton stretched out in the bath, listening to the drip from the tap hit the surface. If ever he needed some time to himself, to stop and reflect, to switch off the world and focus, this was the place.

He heard the bathroom door creak open. Padding footsteps, slippers on the tiles. The heavy wooden toilet seat lid coming down with a crack against the porcelain.

So much for alone time.

On the other side of the drawn shower curtain, Clayton's seventy-three-year-old grandmother, Tuula (or "Firebreather," as his grandfather had affectionately dubbed her), plunked herself down on the toilet seat with a muffled groan. Though he couldn't see her, he knew her left hand held an ever-present lit cigarette. In the bathroom, her habit was to hold it close to the slipstream of air being sucked up into the ceiling by the exhaust fan and away from the aged and highly flammable curtain.

"*Mummu*! Seriously?"

"You don't have anything I have not seen, Clayton. You used to love running all around the house *alasti* as the day you were born."

"You might have noticed I'm not a child anymore, Mummu. I'm eighteen."

"Agh, you will always be a child to me, *lapsi*."

Clayton sighed and sank deeper into the bath, resigned to giving up any semblance of privacy. "It's happening," he said simply.

Tuula blew smoke from the corner of her mouth and frowned. "Ashley is going away?"

"Yeah. For a while."

"Where is she going? When is she going?"

"To America. Publicity tour. Plane leaves Wednesday."

"That is very sudden. It is, what, four days since her record?"

"Yeah. Blythe and her army of droids or zombies or whatever the hell she has working for her got real busy making calls and pulling favors and brownnosing. Ash is going to be doing stuff on TV and radio. Lots of talk shows. Then to some specialist training facility in Colorado for a month."

"For how long is she away?"

"Ten weeks."

"And what flight will you be catching?"

Clayton laughed. "Well, I was going to hire a zeppelin, but I thought a hovercraft was more my style."

"Agh, you make fun," Tuula said. "You can go. You have money you have earned from your comics and your shirts."

"Mummu, I'm no Stan Lee."

"I can give you the rest."

"It's not the money. This is strictly a 'Team Drum' affair."

"What? Team Dumb?"

"Team *Drum*. As in Drummond. You know, Ash, Blythe, Len, Ash's coach, Mr. Dwyer. And the undead publicists Blythe handpicks for these sorts of things."

"Team Drum, Team Drum…*Perkele*." Tuula reached behind her and grasped the ashtray sitting on the back of the toilet. She tapped ash and cleared her throat. "Team Drum is the shit!"

Clayton bit his lip, holding back a laugh. "Mummu, it's just shit," he said gently, "not *the* shit. *The* shit means it's great."

"Great? Shit is great?"

"No, shit is bad. *The* shit is great."

Tuula muttered several phrases in her native Finnish, took a long drag on her cigarette and emptied the smoke via her nostrils. "And *sick*. You were telling me last week this also means great."

"Yes."

"Shit...Sick...How did this happen?"

"I don't know. Somebody started using them that way and they stuck."

"Ya, kids." The woman who had raised Clayton since he was three scratched the part in her grayed bob, then patted the porcelain bowl she sat on. "They turn English into a *vessa!*"

"Maybe we want to keep everyone else guessing."

Tuula grunted, eager to leave behind the linguistic crimes of today's youth, and tacked back to the news of the day.

"Well, you will have the no worries with Ash coming back to you. She is not a devil like her *äiti*. She is a good girl. Very sensible. And the two of you are in love—any *typerys* can see that."

Clayton sat back upright. Though her directness made him uncomfortable, his grandmother had considered her words carefully. She knew a thing or two about love, and she wasn't afraid to call it the way she saw it.

By the time he replied, Tuula was lighting a second cigarette.

"Ash and I are meant to be together," he said. "But things are already changing because of that world record.

And there's more change to come for sure." He exhaled. "I just hope we're meant to *stay* together."

Tuula produced a long grumble from the back of her throat. "You wonder if you are enough for her, yes?" She gave the ashtray in her hand a little shake. "I will help you see. Did I ever tell you about your *isoisä* and the fortune-teller?"

"Yes, of course, Mummu."

"Ay?"

"Yes, I've heard the story about Grandpa and the card reader."

"How many times?"

"Heaps."

"How many?"

Clayton shifted in the water and opened the end of the curtain to peer around at his grandmother. "Fourteen."

"Ha! Not nearly enough!"

Tuula cleared her throat.

"Your isoisä had fallen in love with me. We had met on a tram in Fortitude Valley—he was very handsome in his uniform and his slouch hat. He gave up his seat for me, and we began talking. My English wasn't great—I had been in Australia for one month and five days— but he was very patient. He wasn't like other people who would frown and roll their eyes and treat you like *paska*.

He listened with care. He asked to learn some Finnish. How to say 'You are beautiful.' Well, that's what he wanted me to translate. I actually taught him to say 'I look like a dog's behind.' I didn't correct him until many weeks later. Anyway, by the time we reached Milton, he had asked for my hand in marriage. I said I would like to go to a movie cinema first. We went and saw *South Pacific*, and during the song 'I'm Gonna Wash That Man Right Outa My Hair,' he gave me a kiss on the cheek. That was the first time I thought he could be my *armas*."

Tuula paused to smoke. Clayton smiled in anticipation. Fourteen times he'd heard the story of his grandparents' courtship—fourteen times his heart had raced like a hamster in a wheel. And if the future delivered fourteen more—hell, fourteen *hundred* more—that giddy feeling would accompany Mummu's words every time.

"We had known each other for two months when he asked me again to marry. I didn't want to go to a movie cinema this time. I didn't want to do anything except say yes. But I was confused. Two months is not a long time. How could I be very sure he wasn't a *kusipää*? You know, an arsehole. I wanted a little information, a little guidance. I told your isoisä this, and he said he knew a fortune-teller who could give me the peace of the mind. I didn't think it was true, but I went along anyway because he was paying. The reader was a fat Australian woman.

Her name was Beryl. She told me the man I was seeing was a 'top bloke'; he would make a 'ripper of a hubby' and would never 'shoot through.' He would forever be 'dinky-di' to me. I didn't understand anything this Beryl said, but I knew from her face and from the way she said the words she thought your grandpa was a very good man."

Tuula flicked ash into the tray.

"Then I had a strange thought—I know Beryl! I searched my mind for when and where I had met this fat woman. It was two weeks before, on the tour your grandfather gave me of his barracks. She had been serving food to the soldiers in the messy hall."

"Mess."

"Ay?"

"Mess. *Mess* hall."

"Ay…whatever," replied Tuula, waving her hand. "The important point is, I had seen Fat Beryl before, and she was no fortune-teller. So I asked her if your isoisä had paid the fee. She said, *My oath*, which meant yes. Then I asked her what she had been paid to do. Fat Beryl said she didn't know what I was talking about, but I kept asking until she became red in the face and lowered her eyes. It turned out your isoisä was the cheeky comedian. He had paid Fat Beryl to pretend to be a reader and to say nice things about him! Agh, can you believe it?"

"No way! Never heard of such a thing, Mummu."

"Yet it is true! And when I confront your grandpa, he laughed and said it was only a joke. He said he was sorry if I had been embarrassed. I told him I wasn't the one spending all my money on Fat Beryl. He laughed again and said he knew a man with a crystal ball who could give me proper information. And that's when I decided I must marry your isoisä before he became a penniless kusipää clown." Tuula rose, stubbed out her cigarette. "That is the end. Now I am going to go heat up some *kesäkeitto*. You would like a bowl?"

"Hey, Mummu?" Clayton drummed his fingernails on the rim of the tub. "You said this story would help me see."

"Ay."

"See what?"

Tuula narrowed her eyes and placed her free hand on her hip. "Maybe it's not that you can't see, lapsi. Maybe you just need to open your eyes." Turning on her heel and exiting the bathroom, she added, "Anyway, it is not for me to give you everything like a television show! My job is to tell the stories! Stories that are *the shit*!"

Clayton closed the curtain again and sank back into the bath. He touched his palms to the surface of the water, watching ripples roll out from the disturbance. His grandmother's tales were always funny and poetic and compelling, usually reason enough to listen. But she was quite insistent that today there was a lesson to learn, that some strange brew of wartime Brisbane and *South Pacific* and Fat Beryl could provide insight into the immediate problem of Clayton and Ash and ten weeks of absence.

He turned the story over in his mind, examining it.

Maybe if he stayed in the bath a bit longer, understanding would somehow be absorbed. Maybe he just needed more time to soak it all in.

But the water was getting cold.

Seven

The clearing in the rainforest might have been a paradise found. Twin waterfalls, separated by a jagged spine of rock, plunged down a rhyolite cliff face. In the final meters of the drop, the two streams stretched and divided, the droplets like tumbling diamonds. Beyond the waterfalls, on the track leading back into the forest, grass trees resembled land anemones, swaying to and fro in the gentle breeze. Eucalypts with frayed trunks reached high into the canopy. The bright, hopeful call of a lone Albert's lyrebird floated up from some faraway hollow in the valley.

Ash emerged from a private nook near the waterfall in a pair of boardies and a crop top, her hair down. Clayton watched her skip across the dirt track and onto a flat slab of granite overlooking the water.

"You coming in?"

"I still can't believe that on your day off you want to go swimming."

She pointed to the water-lover ring on her thumb. "No choice." She grinned and dove into the pool below. She spent a good half minute under—enough time for Clayton to gingerly step out over the ledge to check on her—before she burst up from the water with a spray from her mouth and a deep breath in.

"Jesus, Ash. People hurt themselves doing shit like that."

"I checked before I jumped. What, did you think I wasn't coming back up? Did you think I was gonna stay down there?"

He huffed at her, which only made her smile in response.

"I like that you worry about me," she said.

"I don't."

"Uh-huh. Seriously, come on in—it's beautiful."

He watched her effortlessly glide through the water, then float on her back, staring straight up at the sky.

"I know," he said.

He took his shirt off and skirted the walking track, searching for easier access to the swimming hole.

"Chicken."

"The water's cold."

"It's fine."

Clayton held his breath and waded in. The water *was* cold, and he was covered in goose bumps until he adjusted to it. Soon he too lay on his back, arms and legs spread wide, paddling to stay afloat beside Ash. Both of them stared up through the gray-green canopy of eucalypts to a cloudless sky.

"You think I should come to the airport tomorrow?" asked Clayton.

"You're kidding, right?"

"It's going to be a circus, Ash. You know that. Reporters and TV and stuff. Fans. And your mum, of course. She won't let us be together for two seconds."

"It won't be that bad. And for the last time, Mum's not out to get you."

"You're right. She's out to get *us.*"

She flicked water at him. "You're being a doofus."

"Really? Because it seems like a pretty long trip when there are no meets, no competitions. Just ten days of that training camp. What's the rest of the time for?" Ash started to respond, but Clayton spoke over top of her. "I know. I get it. It's so Blythe can show off her world-record holder. Make Ash Drummond a household name. Give the globe a little"—he made air quotes—"*wake*-up call."

Ash paddled to the shallows and rested on the rocks. A dragonfly hovered above her left shoulder for an instant, then flitted away.

"Mum wants the best for me," she said. "All this potential and the opportunities that go with it—she doesn't want any of it wasted. I know she's a difficult person. Okay, yeah, she's a total dick-punch. But she's behind me. She's got my back. And you know what? I respect that. Especially after how it all went bad for her." She inhaled and again held the breath in her finely tuned lungs. Clayton figured twenty seconds ticked by before the air was released. "I'm not going because she wants me to. I'm going because it's right. This is the next step in the journey."

Clayton held his tongue. Ash was making a bunch of crummy media interviews and a swim-training camp sound like something written in the stars. If she thought this trip was the next step in the journey, she was not asking herself about the final destination.

Tired of treading water, Clayton paddled to the shallows next to her. She leaned over and kissed him.

"Things are going to be fine," she said. "Please come to the airport. Mum might be behind me, but I need you *beside* me."

Eight

Ash stepped through the rocks, waving Clayton along after her. The hiking track, narrow and slippery, skirted the cliff face. At the midway point, it snaked through a gouge in the rock that acted as a small viewing place. Securing the refuge was the merged waterfall, little more than an arm's length from the open edge of the track. Ash found a comfortable spot and waited. When Clayton joined her, she pulled him close and kissed him, long and deep. She brought his hand up and placed it on her left breast. Her hand found the front of his shorts.

"What are you doing?" The knotted drawstring on his board shorts came undone. Clayton gently took hold of her wrist and eased her hand away. "There's people around, Ash."

"So?"

He waved his hand toward a group of middle-aged picnickers just visible through the scrub. His silent argument was met with a renewed attack on his board shorts.

"Ash."

"I want to be close to you. With you."

"Here?" Clayton stared, slightly bewildered. Ash was able to maintain her seductive act for a moment before the facade cracked. She lifted her hands from Clay's shorts, brought them together prayerlike, then let them drop to her sides. Her expression collapsed into pale fear and uncertainty.

"Ash? What's up?"

She hesitated.

"What's going on?"

She bit her lip and stared back at him, her gaze level. "I've been thinking a lot about that drawing you did." She didn't say which drawing. She didn't need to. Both of them knew.

"And it made you want to tear my boardies off?"

"Shut up. That drawing. It weirded you out, didn't it?"

"No."

"Come on."

"No. It didn't." Clayton heard her *hmm*, sensed her unflinching stare. "It's different. I'll admit that. I don't usually do creepy watercolors that look like wanky art-school-dropout stuff."

Ash nodded. In the distance, above the thrum of the falls, the Albert's lyrebird continued to cry out for a mate.

"I want to tell you something," she said. "And I don't want you to think I'm completely nuts, okay?"

"I think you're completely nuts anyway."

"Don't." Her tone was grave enough to crush any further joking around. Clayton saw that her hands were shaking. "The day of the world record, did you—" She paused. "*See* anything?"

"Like what?"

She swallowed and took hold of his wrists. "Anything *strange*. While I was in the pool."

Clayton scoured his mind. "No," he replied. "It was the usual scene…up until the scoreboard announcement. Things got bent after that."

Ash looked over Clayton's shoulder. Their small alcove in the cliff darkened as the sun slipped behind the only cloud in the sky. "Have you heard some athletes say they leave themselves during a race?"

"Leave themselves?"

"Yeah. They're so into it that they get out of their bodies."

"Okay. Did that happen to you in the world-record swim?"

She nodded. "It's happened before. I sort of drift above and look down at myself in the water. I watch my stroke, my rhythm. I can spot if I'm moving too stiffly or too loosely. I can see everything."

"All right, I give. That *is* strange."

"I haven't gotten to the strange bit yet. I was about two-thirds into the sixth lap when I felt myself elevating. I looked down and saw myself in the water. I was flawless. There were no tweaks I needed to do, no adjustments I had to make. Everything was perfect.

"I stayed like that, looking at myself for the next two laps, almost all the way to the finish." She squeezed Clayton's hands. "You ready for the strange bit?"

"I guess."

She peeked again at the falls. "My hands and feet. They…"

"They what?"

"They weren't there."

"Come again?"

"I mean, they were there moving like usual. But you could see right through them. It's like they *were* the water."

Clayton felt a chill trickle down his back. The noise of the falls surrounded him, filling his head to the brim.

"You didn't notice?" asked Ash. "I was sure you would've. You know, because of the drawing. The way you blended my hands and feet into the wave. I thought you must've seen something too."

Around them the thin mist wafted like a cold breath exhaled. Their eyes were anchored on each other for an age. Then Ash's fell away.

"I know, I know." She held her face in her hands. "I'm being ridiculous. It's just a coincidence. You did some creepy art. I did a visualization technique amped up to the max. That's it. Nothing to see here—move along."

Her hands slid away, revealing a smile. Clayton could see its fragility.

"Let's go back to yours," she said, standing up. "I could do with a dose of reality."

They ambled out of the small resting place and back onto the worn, sun-drenched trail hugging the cliff face. Nearing the boulders at the rock pool's southern bank, Ash glanced back over her shoulder. The waterfall was a postcard of innocent, harmless splendor.

Nine

Over the twelve hours that followed, Ash and Clayton did not part. They discarded Ash's eerie admission at the falls and drove back to Brisbane in a welcome comfortable silence. He piggybacked her across the threshold when they arrived home, only for her to coax him into turning around and coming in again, with her piggybacking him. They snuggled on the couch for three episodes of *Summer Fall*, arms wrapped around each other until they were uncomfortably warm.

"If this girl was a *laulujoutsen*, a swan," said Tuula of Clayton's iron grip, "she could not fly away. You have stolen too many of her feathers, lapsi."

Later, while Tuula walked to the 7-Eleven for more cigarettes, they made urgent, clumsy love on the living-room rug. A second session of sex, set against the back-drop of Tuula's snores and occasional curses in Finnish from the next room, was slower, less burdened with the following day's weight.

∽

The slipping away began in the morning, after breakfast. A text from Blythe demanded Ash return home to pack. Clayton sat in the passenger seat of the Corvette, feet up on the dash, hand under his chin. At the Drummond house, he stayed at her heel. He wanted nothing to do with either parent, not Len and his small talk laced with New Testament quotes or Blythe and her wordless stare.

Packing provided a brief respite. Within the familiar space of Ash's bedroom, Clayton felt more at ease. She sought his opinion on clothes for TV appearances, he suggested a fat novel for the flight, he organized phone and computer cables and an adapter plug for the North American sockets. He sat on the suitcases as she worked the zips around. At the end of the hour-long exercise, Clayton theatrically wiped his hands.

"I think we're done here."

"Yeah. Although I bet Mum will think of something we've forgotten."

On cue, Blythe crashed the room—no knock, no warning—and barked out commands. "Make sure you've got all Australian tracksuits, not state or club ones.

The medals from the Pan Pacs—bring those. You got those against the Yanks. Did you read the email from Kyla about skirt length for *Good Morning America*? They have strict unofficial guidelines. Are the notes on interview technique packed? Keep them out. You'll need to go over them on the plane."

No stinkeye was leveled at Clayton during the scramble. In fact, Blythe avoided any acknowledgment of his presence. He was relieved. Usually he was a target for Team Drum's dictator, in the crosshairs for a look or a lecture. But here, in Ash's space, things were different. Blythe treated him like a ghost. Was it too much to handle, seeing this dropkick boy in her pride and joy's inner sanctum? The inkling that they shared everything, bed included? Was this—the adult equivalent of holding your breath—really the best way she knew how to deal with her daughter growing up? The answers could only come from Blythe's own downturned mouth. And Clayton wasn't about to ask. In this small corner of their overlapping worlds, he was more than happy to be invisible.

～❦

When Clayton and Tuula arrived at the airport, the scene was more subdued than what Clayton had imagined. The media wasn't overwhelming—two camera crews were on hand, forming a scrum around five or six solo journalists. Although it had become more common for Ash to be stopped in the street and asked for an autograph, the only "fans" come to see her off were opportunistic stickybeaks already at the airport and wondering what the fuss was about.

Around midday the final boarding call for flight 520 to Sydney was announced. Ash wrapped her arms around Clayton, and they held each other tightly. They kissed. Ash's eyes welled with tears, and Clayton's ears and cheeks burned red.

"I'll check your comic every day," she said. "I don't want to see any soppiness. Make them funny."

"I can't be funny on command," he said, shoving his hands in his jeans pockets. "And I'm never soppy. Now bugger off. Get on your flight."

"I love you."

"You're losing your place in the queue."

"You love me too."

"Will you go already?"

"Okay!" Ash smiled. "Don't wait up." She blew him a kiss as she was bundled up and folded into her entourage. The camera lights flickered to life as the reporters conducted brief interviews with Coach Dwyer and Blythe, each going through the motions, before they moved on to the star of the show. A larger crowd began to form, and at its center Ash stood tall, shoulders back, breezily welcoming whatever the United States had in store for her.

"I love you too," said Clayton.

Ten

Clayton stuffed his hands back in his pockets and made his way over to Tuula, who was feigning interest in the nearby souvenir shop.

"Let's get out of here, Mummu."

"You do not want to see her leaving?"

Clayton shook his head. "I've seen it. I mean"—he gestured at the growing circus surrounding Ash—"look at it."

"I am looking, lapsi. And I am seeing. But can you wait just a little?" Tuula squeezed his shoulder. "I am so *janoinen*, I need to get myself some water. I will be back *minuutissa*."

Clayton sat on a nearby bench and stared at the carpet. The faint outline of some long-ago spill was visible beneath his feet. It seemed fitting. He felt as if he were leaking, that the pressure of good thoughts and maintaining positivity was weakening him, cracking him. If he didn't get out of here soon, he might dry up completely.

"Hi, kid."

Clayton lifted his head, unsure if the greeting was directed at him. It was. Coach Dwyer stood before him.

"Mind if I have a quick chin-wag?"

"Um, okay."

"You sure? You need to hit the road?"

"I do, but I can't yet. I'm waiting for my grandmother."

"Well, I won't hold you up for long." He sat beside Clayton on the bench and looked out at Ash's impromptu conference. "Not sure we've ever said much more than hello before now."

Clayton shrugged.

"That's my fault. I'm sorry for that," Coach Dwyer said.

"Why are you sorry?"

"A coach has to know all the things that make his athlete tick—positive and negative. I didn't notice just how close you two were until the record swim, and I probably should have been more proactive." Dwyer smiled and ran a knuckle over a shaggy eyebrow. "She talks about you a lot. In training."

"Right." Clayton was still unsure why he had been drawn into this conversation.

The coach nodded, stared down at the ongoing scrum slowly winding its way toward the customs gate. "I don't agree with any of this dog-and-pony-show rubbish. This trip—it's all the work of Mother Drummond. Cyclone Blythe, I call her. She's blowin' hard for the States. It's unnecessary—it's distracting. It's way too bloody long."

"Yeah, it is."

"At least we get some quality time in Denver. I'll get to fix things up then." Dwyer got to his feet. "I just wanted to let you know that you're real important here, kid. Ash might be the strongest competitor I've ever seen, but she still needs good people around her. She needs you to be with her 100 percent, even if you're an ocean apart."

Clayton nodded. "A hundred per cent," he echoed.

The coach had barely departed when a second person approached. Clayton was all too familiar with this figure, the timing of the greeting a giveaway as much as the voice. Coach, who may not have remembered his name, called him "kid." But only one person ever addressed him as "boy."

"Hello, Blythe." He liked to drag out the vowel in her name, giving it a nasal, country twang.

"Where is your grandmother?"

"Around. Close."

"Of course." Blythe scanned the thoroughfare to her left. "Remarkable woman. Foreigner. English not great. On her own. But here she is, raising a young orphan." Her attention shifted back. "I'm sorry—*orphan*'s not the right term these days, is it? What's the term?"

"I wouldn't know."

"Really?"

"No."

"Hmm…that surprises me."

Clayton held Blythe's stare. Seconds ticked over. A train of baggage trolleys rattled past, towed by a motorized cart. Laughter leaped from the TV crews bidding farewell to Team Drum. Ash's earnest admission could be heard above the din: "I don't know! Maybe it's a surprise!"

"She's ready," said Blythe, smiling again. "From the day she was born, from the first time I dunked her head in the pool when she was a baby, this was inevitable. And where she's going—that's inevitable too. Everything she deserves, it's coming. Ashley Ray Drummond is living her destiny and leaving the past in her wake."

Clayton folded his arms. If Ash had been within earshot, she would have been making gagging motions behind her mother's back. Everything out of Blythe's mouth sounded rehearsed, like she had a camera crew in tow. Everything was an interview.

"She's sensitive, my Ashley," continued Blythe. "Always had a soft spot for the…well…the *less fortunate*. The good old Aussie battler. As a child she would bring home stray dogs from the local pool. No matter how mangy, no matter how pathetic. Yes, compassion is a real strength of hers. And sometimes a weakness." She prodded the surgical scars on her left shoulder. "But the job's done now. It's time for Ash to focus, free of impediment. Free of any dogs she might have picked up along the way."

"Isn't that up to her?"

"It is," said Blythe.

Clayton smelled the lavender and sweat and chlorine emanating from her pores. He noted that, despite all her hours spent in the pool, Ash never smelled of chlorine, and he wondered why that might be.

"But it's too late now," Blythe added. "You know that surely."

"Too late for what?"

Blythe sighed and sat down beside Clayton. He leaned away from her, the look on his face pure sucked lemon. "I want to apologize," she began. "I know that since you started dating my daughter I've been…I think it's fair to say somewhat cool. I was wrong to do that. I should've been more sympathetic, more understanding. *Greet all brethren with a holy kiss,* my dear husband constantly reminds me." She smiled. If she made even the slightest move toward kissing him, Clayton was going to instantly lose his breakfast. "You don't have a mother, of course," she continued. "A real mother. That's sad. Very sad. And I really should've been more understanding of that from the get-go. Oh well, live and learn."

Blythe paused, considering her words. Somewhere in the terminal, a baby was crying.

"I need to help you properly understand who a mother is, what she has to do. First and foremost, a mother has to be the lane ropes for her child. Always keeping them on track, never letting them stray where they don't belong. For so long, you haven't had any lane ropes to guide you. Maybe that's what you're missing."

Blythe lowered her head and leaned in. Her kindly tone slid easily, almost gracefully, into regret. "You need to get out of my daughter's lane, Clayton. Let her go. It's what's best for her. And for you."

"Aargh, lapsi! You are getting too close to a *lohikäärme*! Move away before she sets your hair on fire!"

A startled Blythe jumped up, stumbling briefly on a kink in the carpet, as Tuula moved between them with all the grace of a tank. The old woman held an open bottle of water high, insisting the "dragon" keep its distance.

"Are you okay?" she murmured to Clayton.

"Fine."

"Yes?"

"Yes, Mummu."

Tuula turned and faced Blythe, who had regained a semblance of composure. "You are not in America yet? This is taking a long time."

"We will be there soon enough."

"Yes, yes…I think they will be excited to meet Ash. And I am sure they are holding their breath waiting to meet you too."

Blythe smiled and offered a small round of applause. She winked at Clayton. "You'll do what's best for her. I know you will." Pulling her scarred shoulders back, she turned on her heel and strode back to the departing entourage.

"Goodbye!" shouted Tuula. "And speaking of breath, I found out a large man with a vessa mouth will be sitting beside you on the airplane! He has the body odor too! He will like you, I think!"

Clayton wrapped an arm around his grandmother's shoulders. "Thank you, Mummu."

"For what? This is my job."

"Thank you anyway."

"No problem. You understand—this time will pass."

"Yeah."

"What did that devil say, lapsi?"

Clayton let go, and together he and his grandmother walked to the exit and into the carpark. "She said you were remarkable, Mummu."

"Me?"

"Yeah. Seriously."

"Ah, she thinks I am the shit?" Tuula cleared some phlegm from her throat. "I feel the same way about her."

Eleven

She was all over his social feeds. Site after site, clip after clip. She never lingered long in any one spot, but she was never far away. Sometimes the shows were neatly divided into segments, and the links made her easy to find. Other times he would be forced to jump back and forth through hours of footage, usually for little more than yet another softball, checklist set of questions. Through it all, he collected snatches of programs with no continuity, no context, no understanding of the *key demographic* they courted or the endless parade of *content* they dragged before the camera. Performing terriers, self-help gurus, miracle cleaning products. In slinky Versace outfits chosen by her mother, Ash walked among them, providing five minutes of shark banter here, a joke about Vegemite there. The endless fascination with her physique was ghoulish.

"Your shoulders are extraordinary."

"Do you have to get your clothes tailored?"

"What size shoe do you wear?"

She was careful to translate to US sizes. Everything's bigger in the States, she added. The audience whooped and hollered. Someone chanted, "YOU-ESS-AY! YOU-ESS-AY!"

They called her "beautiful" and a "hottie" and "formidable." They asked her when she knew she was destined to be a swimmer. They debated whether she could beat the current American champ. They suggested she do movies when her swimming career was done. She smiled and nodded and told stories and shared feelings and projected confidence and humility. One presenter introduced her as "*the* Wake." Clayton easily pictured Blythe at the wing of the set, just off-camera, fixing the stare, but impotent. Ash didn't correct the host. No doubt she would later be coached how to do so with appropriate humility. An offhand, crowd-pleasing admonition would be ready for next time.

They called her Ashley Ray, double-barreling her name like Betty Sue.

⊘

Direct communication from Ash began with bundles of excited emails, detailing sights, accents, serving sizes, cars, teeth, expectations of place both confirmed and confounded. She promised to video-call Clayton as soon as possible, despite the difficulties of time zones and schedule. Within a couple of weeks, though, her updates thinned, merely listing the endless engagements as she was shuttled between cities that blurred into the same dull, dry strip. Clayton offered to stay up as late as necessary to make it convenient for Ash to video-call, but she didn't respond. Meanwhile, her public social-media feed continued blaring the sights and fizzing with excitement. Suspicions that someone else was posting these updates was confirmed when "Ash" shared how "fab" the breakfast buffet was at some hotel, taking care to use the hashtag #blessed.

Truth be told, Ash seemed to be struggling. Her only positives were a few precious moments spent in hotel pools. Getting away to a proper facility or the beach or somewhere with real water was out. Too many chaperones, not enough time. Keep smiling. Don't stop.

Clayton's responses—brief recaps of life at home, work on his website, new T-shirt designs, photos, appeals for her to hang in there—fell on deaf ears.

An appearance on *The Late Night Show* offered a chance for a live check-in that he could at least watch on a decent-sized screen. Accompanied by Tuula, Clayton watched the broadcast, perched on the edge of his seat, catching each moment like the last drips from a drinking fountain. Seeing her up close and in high def at first filled him with relief. She walked through the curtain, waved nervously to the crowd and took a seat by the host's desk, her smile bright, her eyes warm. Tuula offered a sidelong nod to her grandson.

"I think she has not yet turned American, lapsi. Her head is still the same size."

She added that Ash looked homesick. Clayton saw it too—and more that his mummu could not. Ash was washed out. And something about the way she moved bothered him. Her typical effortless grace (almost as beautiful through air as it was through water) came across as stunted and stiff. She perched bolt upright on the talk-show couch and gestured thickly as yet again she answered the same half dozen dumb questions. Her voice was hoarse, like she was desperate to clear her throat but couldn't. There were good, rational reasons for this. She was traveling. She was tired. It was hardly surprising that she should be longing for home and weary of the trip and that this should fray the edges of her on-screen presentation.

And yet.

Finally the show's host asked a new question, one Clayton hadn't heard put to Ash before. Did she have a partner?

"Partner?" said Tuula.

"Boyfriend," said Clayton. "Or girlfriend."

"Oh!" cried Tuula, spilling ash from her dying cigarette.

Blythe would most certainly have had a canned reply for just such a question, but the response from Ash was clearly not that. "Well," she said, "I'm pretty sure my bloke at home will be watching this right now. Hi, Clayton!"

A slump of the shoulders and a comical thought-I-was-in-with-a-chance smirk from the host prompted honking guffaws from the audience. Ash shot a half smile right back at the camera and held her hands up in apology.

She was keeping it together, but Clayton could see tiny cracks in the facade. The host threw to the ad break, and the house band knocked out a bluesy version of "Truly Madly Deeply." In the split second before the ad kicked in, the camera captured Ash in a moment she didn't have to be "on." She picked up a mug from the desk and drained it in one greedy hit.

Clayton couldn't sleep that night. The image of Ash in that studio ran on relentless *repeat* in his mind. Something about the odd way she had downed that drink disturbed him. For the briefest of moments, she was a stranger, barely recognizable. The mug in her hand? It was a full canteen found in the desert. She looked frail, like she could crack and fall apart at any moment.

After hours of restless rolling left and right, Clayton finally arrived at the word that perfectly described her. Ash had become *brittle*.

Twelve

No amount of herding between television studios, talks with potential sponsors, free breakfasts, not even a few stolen minutes in an overheated hard-water chemical bath of a hotel pool, could dislodge the image from Ash's mind. Every time she closed her eyes, she saw his face, pale and kissed with tiny air bubbles. He didn't look panicked. He didn't struggle for air. That serene, resigned expression on his face was the part that disturbed her the most.

Could a nightmare haunt you after sunrise?

The terror had first hit her in week four of the trip, somewhere in the desiccated sprawl of Los Angeles. In total darkness and air-conditioned hum, she returned to the day they met. Initially it followed the charted course: Clayton swimming alone in the surf before the tongue of murky brine sent him away from land and brought them together at sea. She watched as he fought the current.

"Hold on, Clay."

His arms dragged more and more as he struggled to keep position. He kicked and raised himself higher. He clawed at the water as he slipped deeper and deeper. Ash watched with alarm as the rip flung him out past the point. She swam toward him, set to intervene, ready to escort him back to shore.

Then the ocean spoke. She heard it when she turned her head to breathe. The voice was assertive. Urgent. Impossible to ignore.

Let go.

The voice pierced her, penetrating deep into her bones. Feeling a sluggishness that was unprecedented in her swimming career, she stopped to catch her breath—a fatal pause. Clayton lifted his arms like a diver signaling descent and disappeared. Ash plunged after him, but it was too late. The ocean had staked its claim. Clayton was beyond reach.

Ash woke up sweating, gasping through a dry mouth, a dull ache pulsing in her feet. The voice echoed in her mind for some time afterward, but it passed. The vision of Clayton drifting away on the current—it refused to budge.

~🌀~

Ash filled the paper cup as fat globs of oxygen rose through the cooler.

"Man, why do they make these so bloody small?"

She drank, crushed the cup and tossed it toward the bin, bouncing it off the rim.

"Your aim a little off?" said Coach Dwyer, clamping a hand on her shoulder.

"Probably."

"It'll be done soon, champ. All this song and dance."

"Yeah."

"Another week and you'll be back doing what you're supposed to do."

Ash nodded and swallowed hard.

"And don't worry too much about the stiffness in your knees—they're just a little out of practice, that's all."

"How did you know about my knees?"

"It's my job to know."

Eagle-eyed though Coach Dwyer was, there was something he couldn't know—the pain had settled in the morning after Ash's first nightmare. More than that, it was mobile, darting from joint to joint, gradually but assuredly spreading wider. At the outset it was subtle, like a bruise deep within the ball of her left foot. The next day it had shifted to the right. Then it vanished from her feet altogether, resurfacing in both knees, behind the knee-caps, buried in the tendons. Ash couldn't explain this moving target of an injury. The best she could come up with was some type of stress embolism, inspired maybe by her disturbed dreams, running rampant through her body. It sounded more like a line from a movie trailer than a medical diagnosis, but professional assistance was out of the question. Seeking help meant sharing the turmoil in her unconscious—that wasn't a conversation she was prepared to have, not even with Coach Dwyer.

No, she would deal with this on her own. What sort of competitor was she if she couldn't push through pain? Ignore it, mask it, minimize it, emerge victorious. That was the distance swimmer's way, Ash Drummond's way. The numbers told her she was better at it than everyone else on the planet.

And as for the nightmare—well, that was just a nightmare, wasn't it? It was a lie. The day she and Clayton met was in the past, fixed in time. The truth of it could never be altered. At some point in the near future, the nightmare would give up and go away. It would sink quietly, leaving no trace behind.

Surely it would.

Thirteen

Clayton worked at his desktop, bathed in the blue glow of a high-resolution screen. He took a deep breath. He could hear from the other side of the wall the *tip, tip, tip* of the leaky shower in the bathroom, each *tip* taking longer to arrive than the last. He was supposed to be editing images, working on his comic. Instead he counted out beats between drips, the dull thuds of water on enamel.

"This is ridiculous."

He stood abruptly, sending his chair sliding back across the floor, and stomped to the bathroom. He wrenched the taps closed and swept his hand across the showerhead to clear it.

Silence.

Back in his bedroom, Clayton sat again at the image he was supposed to be editing, a new character based on his memories of Shaz, the woman at the world-record swim meet. He'd refined an idea for a face with its own center of gravity, threatening to turn itself inside out. It wasn't working out. He was pushing too hard. Although he liked skewering the desperate, deluded certainty of the people he encountered, his characters were always drawn with bemused affection. This one? This one was ugly, angry.

He closed the image, not quite ready to consign it to the trash but close to it. Instead he opened a new canvas and grabbed a stylus and his Wacom tablet.

"Be open to whatever comes," he whispered.

My bloke at home.

"Let your hand go where it wants."

It's raining, it's pouring.

His hand paused. He closed his eyes. He pictured himself back in the stands, felt the baying of the crowd, heard Shaz's ear-piercing whistle. And he saw Ash sitting on the lane rope, hands clapping above her head. Triumphant, content. Filled up. A far cry from the husk now attracting views online.

He opened his eyes and watched the screen as his hand began moving with practiced ease on the tablet. The last thing he wanted to do was repeat the conditions under which *Source01* had been created, but nothing else was working. He couldn't draw, he couldn't focus.

He felt drained of inspiration, hollowed out. At least this freaky freestyle thing was *something*.

I love you too.

Clayton pushed harder, his hand flying faster and faster, causing pixels to color with manic intensity on the vertical screen. The stylus wheeled and dipped, glimpses of order emerging from chaos on the screen. He'd never enjoyed working this way, the gulf between his hand working on one surface and the result appearing on another, but right now the disconnect seemed appropriate. And he could feel something closing in, a burgeoning presence in the room.

Said too late for her to hear.

The moment was tangible, but just out of reach. Clayton threw himself deeper into the sketch—manic curves, lines, switch tool, splotches, splatters—no longer concerned if he was summoning forces better left undisturbed. All that mattered was the bond. Making it real. Holding it tight.

Faster.

Faster!

Crack!

A split formed lengthways down the shaft of the stylus. Clayton's heart pounded. Drips of sweat had fallen on the tablet. He slid his chair back to better take in what had happened on his screen. It wasn't *Source02*.

It wasn't a comic. It wasn't anything. Just manic scratches rendered in pixels.

"Ay."

Clayton jumped in his seat, then turned around. Tuula, dressed in robe and slippers, leaned against the wardrobe.

"You are still up."

"Sorry, Mummu. Did I wake you?"

"No. I wake myself these days." The old woman cleared her throat and nodded toward the drawing. "You have been using your gift. This is good—you have not drawn much lately."

"No, Mummu."

"May I see?"

The woman maneuvered around behind Clayton to better see the screen. She studied the image, tilting her head left and right.

"Ah, *abstrakti*. Abstract. Very strong. Much emotion. A self-portrait, perhaps, lapsi?"

"Maybe."

Tuula waved a hand at the center of the mess. "The eyes in this—they are…what is word…squinting? Just a little bit open, yes?"

Eyes? Clayton couldn't detect a pair of eyes in it.

"They are squinting. Like looking into the sun. Maybe the next one they will be open wide." She nodded at the bed. "No eyes—not even in art—should be open wide at two twenty-four in the morning."

"I couldn't sleep, Mummu."

Tuula nodded. "I understand. I had many sleepless nights when your isoisä was in Korea the first time." Tuula leaned closer. "Do you know what I did?"

"You drew pictures. Same as me."

"Yes, that's right! Have I told you this story before?"

"Yes, Mummu. Many times."

"How many times?"

"Twenty-two."

"Ha! Not nearly enough!"

Tuula sat down on the bed.

"For a while, I thought I would never sleep again. And if I could never sleep again, I would go *hullu*. That would not do. Your isoisä would find a madwoman at home when he returned. And he was already crazy enough for the two of us. So I needed to find a way to calm my mind.

"I drew pictures of the two of us. Not in Australia. Not of the times that were real, like when we met or when we got married or when we bought this house. I drew us as children, doing things together in my hometown of Kotka. Riding bikes. Playing with the neighborhood dog. Fishing. Snowshoeing. In every picture, your isoisä was smiling and happy and comfortable. Natural.

When I drew him skiing, he had perfect form. When I drew him skating, he had perfect balance. When I drew him running, he looked like Paavo Nurmi and Lasse Virén. He belonged. He was safe.

"I thought about the drawings many times. I had questions I wanted answered. Why did I go back to the past? Why did I make him...what is word?...*protected*. Why did I make him so *protected*? Was it because he was away at war? Was it just chance? For many years I did not know. Then one day the pictures and I were old and faded, and I understood—it was not my place to question the art. I was meant to be obedient, to be a good soldier. And in the time your isoisä was away, I was a good soldier. I gave myself to the drawings. I was their servant. Doing it over and over, until my hand ached and my neck was sore and my *perse* was numb. Until my energy was gone. And when my energy was gone, my eyes closed and I rested without the crazy thoughts."

Tuula lapsed into silence for several seconds, then clapped her hands. "How is your energy now this is done?"

"Yeah, okay. Now I feel tired," he said, suppressing a yawn.

"Ay, the pencil thing is mightier than the bad thoughts! How wise is your mummu!"

"I think it was your story that did it."

"Cheeky boy. My stories are the shit! I will ignore your comment and go to the vessa now—when I come back I want to see you in bed and snoring like your isoisä used to." She kissed Clayton on the head and exited the room, humming a traditional Finnish tune.

Clayton considered the screen again. Self-portrait? Where did Tuula get that? He couldn't see it. Not even with a squint. He hit the Sleep button. Lights out. Under the covers. The *tip, tip, tip* of the shower had started up again. Less bothered second time around, he decided to count out the sounds. He got to seven before sleep took him under.

Fourteen

Ash climbed out of the Pepsi Elite Swim Center's main pool and took the chamois from Coach Dwyer. As she patted herself dry, she tried to focus on her mentor's feedback.

"Stay off the lane rope…Maybe use more six beat kicks in the middle third…Swimming at altitude is always hard…"

Sentences ran together until all that remained was a steady stream of noise. Her head was elsewhere. In two other spaces, to be precise. The first was a happy place. She was swimming again. Properly swimming. Not in chintzy hotel waders, where the water was more listless than the guests and the excessive chlorine made you feel like a dipped sheep. This was real. This was her element. At first glance, her days were once again simple and recognizable, free of green rooms and guest protocols.

The second distraction was less pleasant. The harrowing daytime visions of Clayton drowning—she'd taken to calling it a "lightmare"—continued to hound her. Eating breakfast, working out at the gym, studying footage of past races. The ghoulish show was apt to strike her at any time. Even the pool wasn't off-limits. Midstroke or during a tumble turn, flashes of his serene, dead face sent her heart rate jumping and her technique astray. More and more it seemed her previous assertion of *it will pass* was wrong. Relief required effort on her part. Something needed to change.

The logic seemed obvious as she lapped up and down the lane, the black line on the pool floor crystallizing her thoughts and pointing the way forward. By the time she was drying off, she'd made her decision.

"Hey, champ, you okay?"

Ash emptied her mind and smiled.

"Yep. I'm good, Coach."

"You sure? Your skin's still pretty wet. Were you sweating in there?"

"No, sir."

"I know it's tough getting back into it after all this TV horseshit. Hitting the water again. It's hard."

Ash handed the chamois back. "Nah. It's the easiest thing in the world."

～◎

She stared at her watch. For the tenth time, she checked the time difference between Denver, USA, and Brisbane, Australia. Finally satisfied, she lifted the phone from her pocket. She couldn't shake the imagined response from her mind.

I can't believe you're doing this to me.

After everything we've been through.

"Keep going," she murmured to herself.

You ambush me like this?

Do I mean nothing to you after all?

"Follow the black line."

As Ash punched out the number, she crossed her fingers that Clayton wouldn't answer. That would be a long shot—Clayton never answered the landline— but it would be just her luck for him to break his habit this once. She *really* didn't want to speak to him.

She wanted to talk to Tuula.

That evening sleep came easily and without dreams. The following day, the "lightmare" abated too.

The image of her man—lifeless, drifting away from her before sinking to the seafloor—would never again hijack Ash's mind.

Fifteen

A thick fog hung in the wattles and white figs lining the street. It did its best to hide the lingering evidence of the flood that had swallowed the suburb twelve months earlier, but telltale signs were still apparent. A mud-encrusted hubcap at the foot of a mailbox. A birdbath lying on its side in a front yard. A once-white garage door now a permanent silty brown. These signs were not lost on Clayton. He chose, though, to view them with a positive eye. The people here—they were tough. They never bowed to the rising waters. They didn't drown.

He hadn't heard from Ash, but that was okay too. In her last message she had sounded more upbeat than she had in weeks. She was finally back in the pool, and she sounded more like her regular self. They had to make the most of their days now—she and Coach Dwyer. It was only reasonable that she wouldn't get too much downtime.

He could wait.

Clayton pushed a hand through his hair and stepped onto the concrete path running parallel to the riverbank. Not even Tuula's weird act this morning could break his mood.

"So, Mummu, we're here for a walk?"

Tuula took a last drag on her cigarette and flicked it into a nearby bin. "Ay."

"A *walk*?"

"Yes."

"At seven thirty in the morning?"

"You have to remind me of this, lapsi?"

"Yeah, I do. You hate waking up early. You hate exercise. I can see you're not enjoying this one bit. What's the deal?"

Tuula muttered several Finnish expletives, then stopped. She gave her hip a rub and belched into her free hand. "Okay, you have found me out. We are not here to make me boobylicious."

"Booty."

"Ay?"

"*Booty*licious."

"My booties need to be licious?"

"Mummu, forget it. What's going on?"

Tuula looked around, then held her grandson by the shoulders. "Ash called me."

He blinked. "She called."

"Ay."

"You."

"Ay, lapsi."

"When?"

"On Thursday. While you were out."

Time difference, thought Clayton. She'd mixed up the times. Easy enough to do. He swallowed. The humid air had a faintly sour tang.

"What did she say?"

"She said a few things, one thing that was very important. She said she had heart change? A changed heart?"

"A...change of heart."

"Ay! That is right." She dropped her hands from Clayton's shoulders and smiled sadly. "She said she had a change of heart."

The blood drained from Clayton's features.

Change of heart.

Change. Of. Heart.

A burning indignation sparked in him. *She spoke to Tuula? Tuula? Who does that? Who breaks up with someone through their grandmother?* Deep down, he'd known this was coming. Blythe had finally gotten to her, convinced her to ditch him from her lane. And she'd agreed. She'd let go. He wanted the river to rise as it had a year ago, as it had thirty-five years before that. He wanted to hitchhike on a passing raft of flotsam to be carried off to the bay. Screw this. Positivity could go to hell.

Tuula's face fell as she watched Clayton come to the boil.

"Oh, perkele paska."

"What?"

"There are times," she said, "when I hate my stupid tongue and my stupid English. There are times when I need more words. Better words."

"*What*, Mummu?"

"Turn around."

Clayton grunted and turned.

Ash was there on the path, in jeans and one of his tees, no more than twenty meters away. Softened by the fog, she looked delicate, weightless. She was paler than when she had left, but her wide smile was undiminished. Clayton walked over to her, and they stood face to face.

"What happened?"

"I wasn't getting what I needed over there."

"You left?"

"I did."

They embraced, reacquainting themselves with the feel of each other. For both of them, it was like slipping out of cold air and into a warm bath.

"Nice T-shirt."

"You'd be amazed how often I hear that. I tell everyone I bought it from this cool webcomic site."

They remained clinging to each other, neither daring to let go.

"Blythe must be thrilled you're here," said Clayton.

Ash groaned and released herself from the embrace. "Beyond words. Actually, *not* beyond words. She had a few choice ones. *I can't believe you're doing this, you ambushed me, do I mean nothing to you?*...I told Mum straight, before we left. She couldn't keep me there. She never thought I would test her out."

The ropes failed, thought Clayton. Now Ash is swimming outside her lane.

"Excuse me, *rakastavainen*," said Tuula, clearing her throat. "I will be going now. This girl made me get up too early. I will go home and get back into bed."

Ash wrapped her arms around Tuula. "Thank you."

"Ay."

Clayton escorted Tuula back to the car. After his grandmother's departure he returned to find Ash seated on a bench near the river's edge. He sat beside her and laid a hand on her thigh. She rested her head on his shoulder.

"So you missed me then?" he said.

"I did."

"I saw your TV stuff."

"Yeah." Ash sighed. "God, some of it was awful."

"The shows were awful. You were great."

"Don't suck up to me, Clayton. That's what Mum's minions are for."

"You did look a bit awkward sometimes."

"I was more than awkward. I was *wrong*. Like... like..."

"A fish out of water?"

"Funny." Ash smiled wanly but quickly dropped the facade. "That whole time we were traveling, I wasn't swimming. And I was scared. Not nervous or anxious. Scared. I didn't know what might happen if it went on much longer. It was like I was in withdrawal. And the nightmares..." She let the sentence trail off.

"You're here now. Things will be better."

"They already are."

Clayton touched the ring on Ash's finger. "Welcome home, water lover."

Sixteen

Clayton watched Ash climb into her jeans and then peek out the window.

"Storm's coming from the west," she said. "Might need an ark to get downtown."

"You have to go?"

She pulled a face. "Yeah. Press conference Mum's set up. Wouldn't be wise for me to stuff her around again after the last few days."

"No, I guess not." Clayton sat up straight, back against the headboard of the bed. He watched Ash lace up her sneakers. "Tell Blythe the stray dog's still around."

"What?"

"Never mind."

Ash frowned, then looked around the room. "Keys?"

"There."

"Thanks." She paused and smiled at Clayton. "Before I go, I have to tell you this. I met a couple on one of the talk shows—they were guests too. When they were young the guy went off to the Vietnam War—he was, like, seventeen, and I think she was fifteen. He went through all sorts of shit there, not surprisingly. He saw his mates get blown up by hand grenades in, like, the first week. Then he almost died in an attack near some creek. The doctors wanted to amputate his legs, but he wouldn't allow it.

"When he got back to the States, the girl's family had moved and he couldn't find her. They ended up getting married to other people. The girl—the *woman*—she got divorced twice. The bloke left his first wife and lost his second to cancer. And when the obituary came out, the woman—she was in her late fifties by now—she happened to be looking for him online and came across it. She got in touch, and when they met again it was like the forty-two years hadn't even happened. He played her the song he'd written for her back when they were kids. They got married. And now they're living happily ever after."

Clayton whistled. "That's some story."

"Word. And you know what my first thought was when I heard that story?"

"What?"

"I thought, That's our story too. We would be with each other, no matter where, no matter when."

She kneeled on the edge of the bed. He leaned over, cupped the back of her neck and laid his forehead against hers.

Thirty minutes after Ash departed, Clayton wandered into the kitchen. Tuula's old radio was on—she preferred local AM and didn't appreciate it when Clayton changed stations. He drank coffee through a news update and a few old tunes before an announcer spoke.

"*Coming up in the next hour we've got a live press conference with Australian swimming's golden girl, Ash 'Wake' Drummond.*"

He sat at the kitchen table and flicked through his feed. Some replies and likes, but no new purchases. He followed a few links and listlessly scanned through walls of memes and GIFs, paying little attention. It occurred to him that this would be their future. They were making it right now—Ash about to speak at a press conference, Clayton working on his craft. There would be more tours, more fame, more separation. But they would always be there for each other.

He had drained his cup and began to make another when the radio broadcast again caught his attention.

"We're a few minutes away from that press conference with Wake Drummond, and for anyone who has been living under a rock and needs a reminder, we've got the live call of Ash's world-record swim two months ago. Here are the final laps. The caller is Mark Cannon..."

Clayton smiled and opened his sketching app to a blank canvas. With his index finger, he began idly marking the tablet screen.

"Drummond is really asking the question now. Look at the kick, that silken turn. It really is something to behold. The race is now for second. Ash Drummond has absolutely slaughtered the field here."

Clayton zoomed in and switched tools to work on some of the textures. He used the watercolor brush. He dabbed at the image, throwing uneven blotches of blue and green to effect just the right tone.

"The only competitor now for Wake Drummond is that world-record line, and, ladies and gentlemen, she is still in front of it!"

He used the ink tool to shape the long tendrils of hair into just the right delicacy.

"WORLD RECORD! Ladies and gentlemen, you will remember this day!"

Clayton blinked as if waking from a dream and zoomed back out to consider the picture in its entirety.

The setting was the same, the texture of the water almost identical. Ash's posture, though, had changed. She was still pictured from behind, but her arms were planted on her hips instead of reaching out. Her legs were wider apart. She was pushing back against the tide.

And failing.

The blending of her extremities with the water had spread. Her body was an outline, still visible but not distinct.

Clayton frowned, turning the device this way and that.

No matter where, no matter when...

Leaving the page open, he pushed the chair back. It teetered for a second on its back legs, then toppled to the floor. He scrambled across the kitchen, desperate for his phone.

The radio announcer returned. "*Well, it seems there's been a delay with the Wake Drummond interview. Not sure if there's a problem, but we'll update you on that as information comes to hand.*"

Seventeen

Her senses were sharp, heightened by adrenaline. Loose, damp gravel pressed into her cheek. Shards of glass pocked her twisted torso. A thin stream of fluid, bright green, fell from what remained of the engine and pooled near her shoulder. She wanted to move, to push herself up off the road, but her mind opted for reason over motion.

How did I get here?

Hands on the steering wheel. Text explosion. A message from Mum.

No farther back.

Kissing Clayton.

Wait, is Clayton here too? Is he okay?

She closed her eyes. Opened them again. Clayton was back at home. Her phone rang, the sound either in her head or out somewhere in the world beyond gravel and glass. The message from her mother—had she tried to read it? Had that been the distraction? No. She'd kept her eyes on the road. What she could see of it anyway.

It had been raining. Pouring. That western storm had come in, all right. Centimeters in minutes. Fat drops had blatted the windshield. Feverish wiper blades had done their best to flick them away. There'd been split-second blindness, pangs of panic.

This debriefing wasn't helping. She squeezed her eyes shut and gently lifted her head. Pain flowered in her neck and down her back. She waved her outstretched fingers around. The ringing phone. She wasn't imagining it— she could hear it. Only in one ear, but she could hear it. She had to find it. She looked around for a sign of it. Nothing.

She needed to move. And to move, she needed to narrow her consciousness down to a single thought: keep going. With a deep breath, she pushed the pain away, as far down as she could manage. She carefully placed her hands flat against the road surface and pushed.

Keep going.

No pain. She pushed harder. She felt okay, strong even.

Keep following the black line.

It was like in the eight—localize the pain, acknowledge it, understand it, set it aside. Never deny the pain, just leave it out of reach. It was working. She took hold of the hurt in her arms, shoulders and neck. Her back. But not all the way down. Strange. No pain in her legs either. In the eight, the legs were last to feel it.

"Oh. Oh Jesus. Hey, are you okay?"

Ash startled, so lost in her thoughts she hadn't noticed the sound of footsteps running toward her. *The phone,* she said. Only she didn't say anything. The words formed in her mouth and stopped. Somewhere between intention and reality.

"Oh shit, I gotta call somebody." A panicked male voice.

Clay. Call Clay. Still no words.

"Hello? Yeah. We need an ambulance. A girl has totaled her car in the storm…"

Ash relaxed her arms and lowered herself back onto the road. Onto the pool floor.

Keep going.

Keep.

Going.

Blue

Eighteen

**ASH "WAKE" DRUMMOND CRASHES CAR,
IN CRITICAL CONDITION**

Champion swimmer and current world-record holder
Ash Drummond has been hospitalised after a car
accident in Brisbane's western suburbs.

The car veered off a stretch of Ellsworth Road in
wet conditions shortly after 2:00 PM yesterday. Police
say nineteen-year-old Drummond was thrown from
the driver's seat after overcorrecting a turn and rolling
the vehicle.

The swimming prodigy, dubbed "Wake" for her
devastating finishing kick, has been admitted to intensive
care at St. Sebastian's. The extent of her injuries has not
been revealed, though her condition is listed as critical.
A source close to the family said that damage sustained

to her spine remains the biggest concern. When asked if the Olympic hopeful's career was over, the source declined to comment.

A formal statement from doctors is expected later today.

The accident has sent shockwaves through the wider community, with athletes, fans, celebrities and the general public flocking to social media with messages of disbelief and support for Drummond and her family. In a brief interview during her morning treadmill session, the prime minister said she was "shattered" by the news and was "praying along with the rest of the nation for Wake's full and speedy recovery."

Many have recalled the chronic shoulder problems and failed reconstructions that ended the promising athletic career of Drummond's mother, Blythe, at a similar age. Some have gone so far as to suggest the family is cursed.

But ABC sports commentator Ziggy Moore angrily responded to suggestions of a Drummond jinx.

"This is nothing more than a tragic coincidence. The lowlifes claiming some sort of voodoo is behind these poor people's misfortunes should be rounded up, taken out to sea and thrown overboard," he said in a blog post this morning.

Nineteen

Silence was never absolute. Machines beeped. Someone was always watching television, though the canned laughter did nothing to drown out the groans and grumbles that punctuated life on a ward. *You need to rest, dear.* How many times had she heard that? How could anyone actually rest in this place?

Darkness was never complete. Low lighting aided the twilight walkers—the oldies who couldn't get through a night without a few pit stops—but it did nothing for someone in need of a decent sleep. Closing her eyes made no difference. The light was burned into her retinas, along with a parade of smiling, encouraging faces. Friendly faces in unfriendly circumstances. There was something false, something desperate in them— doctors and health professionals who didn't know her or only knew her from television, her father (between his rosaries), Coach Dwyer, even Tuula.

You'll be all right.

You'll come out of this stronger.

You're young. You still have your whole life ahead of you.

You're so lucky.

Ash recalled a conversation she had heard backstage on one of the talk shows. Two executive types by the donut table, talking about a colleague. *He'll be gone by the end of the week,* one guy said.

When people start reassuring you, you know you're screwed, said the other.

Sitting up in a hospital bed, supported by a tower of pillows, surrounded by friendly faces, Ash's entire existence was now nothing but reassurance. She was lucky. She would be all right.

Clayton mirrored Ash's preferred silence. Initially he had clung to the same clichés as everyone else, but then he saw the words bouncing off her like tennis balls. So he became silent, still. He held her hand and her gaze with a level-headed calm. His smile was subtle. At low points Ash became irritated with his saintlike demeanor.

When she pushed him away, he took a deep breath and gave her space. When she clawed at his arm in desperation, he stayed beside her.

～◎

Ash heard her mother in the corridors. Everyone heard Blythe in the corridors. Grunting, stamping. Raging. She was disgusted that Ash might not be placed in a private room. She was appalled at the suggestion that a wheelchair was inevitable. She was insistent in her belief—her *absolute certainty*—that her daughter would walk again.

But Ash never saw her mother. Blythe never set foot in the room. She was present and absent. When they wheeled in the temporary chair, Blythe Drummond was nowhere to be found.

～◎

The staff was good. They apologized for the wheelchair's cheap cracked vinyl and flaking chrome veneer.

"You'll be fitted out for something more suitable soon."

Soon was three days. Gleaming and flawless, her permanent chair was a marvel of engineering. Ash regarded it with detached curiosity.

In physio, she felt more at home. This was something familiar—a hard-nosed trainer pushing her to the brink.

You're a champion! Check out the strength in those arms! You're like a gymnast on the high bar!

Ash smiled, but she didn't reply. She didn't feel much like talking. It concerned the medical team and Coach Dwyer. It urged her father to additional prayer, if that was possible. They discussed a depression diagnosis openly, as if she wasn't there.

She wasn't depressed.

She spent a lot of time thinking about swimming, how controlled it was. How contained. When the black line ended, you had two choices: tumble turn and head back in the opposite direction, or stop. She couldn't do either anymore. But where many saw tragedy, Ash sensed opportunity.

When the black line ended, who said you couldn't keep going, right out of the pool, through the earth and into some big wide-open blue?

Twenty

Clayton watched her from a distance, partly concealed by the nurses' station as Blythe stared at the backlit bottles in the vending machine. Ash had once told him her mother drank nothing but bottled water, believing city water to be unclean. Clayton wondered whether the real reason was that city water had no sponsorship potential.

Blythe gave the machine a shove, leaning heavily into it, pushing it back against the wall. She kicked once, twice. She switched legs for a third attempt. The water bottles remained unmoved. Blythe rolled her shoulders, jutted her chin and walked back up the corridor. Clayton thought of turning away, then stepped into the open.

"Oh. It's you, Clayton."

"Clayton? Not 'ComiCon' or 'Boy'?"

"What?"

"You used my name."

Blythe waved a dismissive hand. "Ashley—what's she been telling you?"

"You could ask her yourself."

She reared back a little. "I am *defending* my daughter! She needs to be up and doing more physio, she needs to be in the pool. These doctors are clueless."

"They told me she's still in danger of infection. They said rehab takes months, sometimes years."

"They don't know her. Not like I do. I'm her mother. I've heard them talking about depression. Depression! Ash Drummond! Are they insane? Do they have any idea who they're dealing with?" Blythe leaned back on her heels, balance regained. "This is a blip. A slight detour. We're not going to give up because of some accident and all the losers who want to kneel at its feet."

Clayton raised an eyebrow at her capacity for denial, her complete rejection of reality. A pang of compassion tugged at him. "Why don't you just go in and see her?"

Blythe shook her head, slowly at first, then with more vigor. "Someone needs to play the long game. I know her. Nobody knows her like I do. Nobody." She jabbed a finger at a window by the nurses' station that overlooked the city. "There are billions of people in this world that need someone to believe in. The world needs heroes.

And we have one right here. I don't expect things to go back the way they were before the accident. I expect things to go forward. Better than ever."

Twenty-One

At first Ash's progress was remarkable.

Work began on the floor—stretches and upper-body work and what looked like a whole lot of rolling around. Then the transfers, bed to chair, floor to chair, chair to chair. Ash felt the difference, the confidence in moving, taking control. From the transfers she progressed to the parallel bars, holding herself stiffly and willing her legs to approximate natural movements without bearing weight. Her fitness and age were clear factors in her favor, and she took to the program with the single-mindedness of the elite athlete she was.

Soon, though, her recovery slowed. She faltered more and more on the parallel bars. Heaving herself from surface to surface was hard. Occasionally she wouldn't bother with transfers at all, preferring to stay in her chair.

She began skipping rehab sessions altogether. Her bones ached. Her skin was like parchment.

She missed the water.

Then, five months and twelve days after the accident, a few stiff, twitchy movements in Ash's calves sent excitement prickling through Team Drum. Wake was on the comeback trail. Blythe was triumphant. The physios and nurses were impressed. The doctors wrote more often on their charts. Len talked of recovery instead of divine intervention.

Ash didn't bother correcting them. It was good to put a smile on their faces. But Ash sensed this wasn't improvement.

This was change.

Coach Dwyer took a long, deep breath and regarded Clayton with a heavy-lidded gaze. He'd aged alarmingly in the last few months.

"Yeah, I'm concerned for her," he said, as though considering the question for the first time. "She's in the wilderness. A lot of athletes go through this when their careers end. Maybe not as extreme. But, you know, I'm seeing some signs in her. Real good signs."

Clayton squinted and twisted his mouth to one side. After a year and a half of Ash's media management, he knew a rehearsed statement when he heard one. "Come on, Coach."

"We have to stay positive, kid. I see flashes of her old self. You do too, don't you?"

Clayton nodded, but he knew as well as Coach Dwyer that those flashes faded fast.

Coach shrugged. "I don't know, son. I don't know what more we can do. This accident, it's rocked her. All she's ever been is a swimmer. Now she has to find out who she is all over again."

"She doesn't need to find out who she is," said Clayton.

Dwyer frowned and scratched his ear. "How so?"

"She *knows* who she is. She needs to get back in the pool."

"You don't want to start sounding like Cyclone Blythe, kid."

"I'm not talking about competing. I'm talking about what she *needs*. She's pale and thin. Her mouth is always dry, and she's irritable. She's *brittle*. When she did the talking circuit in the States, it was the same. She needs the water, Coach. I don't exactly know why she needs it so bad"—he paused, trying to think of reasons and failing—"I just *know* she does."

Clayton thought the coach might recommend he do a stint in hospital himself. Dwyer's response, though, made his heart jump.

"What would you like me to do, kid?"

"Talk to the physios, Coach. They won't listen to me, and they *definitely* won't listen to Blythe. You can convince them that this would be good for her."

Dwyer stroked his chin. "This is what Ash wants?"

"For sure."

"I'm worried she'll be set up to fail."

"This isn't pass or fail. This is destiny."

Dwyer smiled at him, an awkward grimace that suggested *destiny* wasn't an expression he used much. "Love the passion, kid. You're a good friend to Ash. And I tell you, after the marriages I've been through, never underestimate the importance of having a good friend as your partner. She's lucky to have you looking out for her."

Twenty-Two

Ash moved off the chair and heaved her lower half to the water's edge. Easing in, she felt nothing, nothing, nothing. Then the glorious, cool touch of quicksilver, at the top of her thighs and groin. She closed her eyes and sighed. Seconds later she was in the center of the pool, floating on her back, hands gliding along the surface, ripples let loose like doves from a cage. A group of elderly women at the shallow end moved awkwardly to some disco tune. Ash paid no attention. She stretched her arms, laid her head back. As the water rushed into her ears, filtered sunlight from the ceiling's skylight warmed her face. The ring on her thumb winked like a tiny lighthouse.

Floating in the water—cradled in its gentle sweep— Ash felt as complete as she ever had. Her spinal column was a footnote.

"Thank you," she whispered.

She wasn't sure exactly who she was talking to.

~◎

Conversation seeped through the thin walls separating the deck from the viewing area. Clayton could visualize the scene without difficulty—Blythe holding the rolled-up brochure in her sweaty hand, its gloss faded from too much contact, patches of ink rubbed away from being carried around for days at a time and laid out every ten minutes for some willing—or unwilling—person to see.

"What do you mean we can't do it?" she cried. "She's made it to the pool. Now is when we push to the next level."

She would be waving the brochure in the specialist's face, causing him to blink. Perhaps she had it open, trumpeting technical specifications. The twin magical therapies: electric stimulation to the spinal cord to encourage regrowth, and a walking-machine contraption from which a strapped-in Ash would hang from an overhead frame, her feet on a treadmill. It would release her from the wheelchair that limited her belief. It was the next logical step.

"There's no point, Mrs. Drummond."

"No point? This will get her walking again!"

"We don't have access to those machines."

"And I've told you a hundred frickin' times already, we can get the sponsorship dollars. It's not a problem. You organize it, I'll get you the money."

"It's not the money, Mrs. Drummond."

"Then what the hell is it?"

A pause. Clayton bowed his head. *They won't work.*

"These therapies are not suited to Ash's injury."

"What?"

"They won't get her walking again. Those machines are effective for people with very different injuries to Ash's. It's been six months now. This is her recovery."

"Are you telling me this is as good as it gets? Is that what you're saying?"

"I'm saying this is her recovery."

Blythe began to pace back and forth, each step a stake piercing the ground. "You've never worked with anyone like Ash before, have you?"

"I have worked with elite athletes, yes," countered the specialist. "From the time of her injury, your daughter has made tremendous progress, Mrs. Drummond. She's regained a lot of function. But there's only so much the body can do to heal itself, electrical stimulation or not. She will not walk. But she can be a champion again. Whether she wants that is up to her."

"There are places that will do this for her," railed Blythe. "We can take her there."

"There are places that will tell you anything if your throw enough money at them, but all they're peddling is false hope."

Blythe let out an exasperated shout. "She's trained her whole life for greatness! And you're giving up! You, a no-name quack, unfit to share the same space as her!"

"Mrs. Drummond, insulting me certainly isn't going to help your daughter. No one is giving up on her. But she needs time to take stock before moving forward. She needs to rest for a while. Find some peace."

Clayton watched Ash roll over, positioning herself to glide. She began to swim. Her hands carved through the water with practiced efficiency, relaxed but in a perfectly held shape.

Even without assistance from her legs, she lifted her body out of the water with each stroke. She touched the wall, turned and made her way back to the middle of the pool before once more rolling over onto her back.

"Hey," he called out.

"Hey yourself."

"Having fun?"

Ash took a mouthful of water and blew a fountain straight up. "You know it."

"Are you okay?"

"Come in."

"I haven't got my togs."

"Suit yourself."

"Ash."

"Yep?"

"Are you okay?"

She continued floating, staring straight up. Clayton waited a while for an answer, then turned away from the pool edge.

"Yeah," she said after him. "I'm good."

The familiar tone skewered Clayton. He turned back and watched her closely, echoes of the twin falls in his ears.

They were there moving like usual.

You could see right through them.

There was fear in that tone, but also acceptance, like she had decided on a course from which there was no escape.

"Let's see where this goes," added Ash.

It was like she was answering another question. One she had posed to herself.

Twenty-Three

The room, lit only by a series of track lights snaking across the ceiling, was a temple of excellence. Dozens of trophies occupied a shelf spanning the full perimeter of the space. A variety of hooks and screws strained under the weight of medals, the overwhelming majority of them gold. Photographs hung on the walls, the older shots featuring a young woman with broad shoulders and a steely gaze. In the newer ones a girl clearly from the same bloodline stood with those same broad shoulders but with a face softened by a lopsided smile and a less forbidding stare. Newspaper and magazine headlines bellowed at each other from their frames. *Teen Sensation Stuns Champ! Move Over Madam Butterfly! Ash Drummond—The Next Big Thing! Wake Leaves Field For Dead!* The loudest shout was reserved for a double-page *West Coast Digress* spread that showed Ash propped up on a massage table in Denver, her feet in the foreground, the block title booming overhead: *WORLD AT HER FEET!*

Blythe checked that the door was locked. Her focus was not on the shrine of success, but on a small photo in her hand, one she'd opted a while back to keep for herself rather than pin up with past glories. It showed mother and daughter post-world-record swim, Ash down on one knee, the two of them touching foreheads. Blythe twisted and turned the print as if it were a shifting hologram.

A lifetime ago now.

Time passed, and Blythe continued staring at the image. She always had to wait before anything happened. It began with a burning sensation in her chest, the sort she would usually suppress. Not now though. Not here. Instead, she let the feeling fester. And it grew. It branched out through her chest and engulfed her heart. It speared her abdomen and clawed its way up her neck, sending a red rash across her face.

A single sob skewered her, enough to tip her over the edge of despair. For several minutes she bent over, huddled with a great squall of pent-up tears that just wouldn't come.

"It's not fair. This is not bloody fair."

Still bent over, she curled her free hand into a fist and waved it around, lashing out at phantom enemies, the evil forces that had torn her down, her and her child. They would not get away with it.

"No," she murmured. She said it again. And again. Each time she spoke, the intensity and volume lifted. The final refute—the tenth—was a scream frightful enough to curdle blood. She shifted her attention back to the photo, to her husband's presence in the background, his eyes skyward, hands together in joyful prayer.

"Where was your God? Huh? When she was caught in the storm? When she was lying on the road?"

She tore the photo in half, crumpled the piece containing Len and threw it across the room. A gasp escaped her mouth as her shoulder recoiled from the sudden thrust. She gritted her teeth as the pain bloomed, withered and died. A prod of the surgical scar and several shrugs brought muscles and ligaments back into alignment. Blythe wiped the perspiration from her upper lip and perched on a stool, facing the shrine. She folded the photo, placed it in her pocket.

"We're not done," she hissed. "We're *never* done."

Blythe stood, took a deep breath, wiped the tears from her eyes and unlocked the door. As she crossed the threshold, she flipped a switch at the wall. The lights went out in the temple.

Twenty-Four

Ash wedged her wheelchair into the open driver-side door of the car, ensuring she was parallel to the seat. With a combination of effort and caution, she lifted herself out of the chair and eased in behind the steering wheel. She considered leaving her legs dangling, then relented, hoisting them over the threshold and depositing them under the foot pedals. Inside the cab, the smell of leather interior mingled with the odors of the closed garage— grease and dust and insect spray and old upholstery. An aged fluorescent tube buzzed and flickered above the Corvette.

Everything was different, down to the last detail. Red luminous dials on the dashboard. Suede steering-wheel cover. Gold knob on the gearstick. The starkest difference between then and now was the body paint. The previous car had been gray—the same hue as the storm clouds that had overseen her near-fatal crash. The vehicle she sat in today? It was blue. She'd requested it.

Ash pretended to shift through the gears, then leaned back, arms folded. The silence was deafening. Nobody ever ventured this far back on the Drummond property. The garage was an outpost, a distant colony for junk and stale air. And the vintage muscle car. Blythe had banished it here. *I do not want to see it. Ever,* she'd said. She couldn't understand why Ash had wanted the car rebuilt. Ash didn't bother to explain. It was a visceral thing. The car ought to rise from the accident, ought to be elevated to a new glory.

She looked to the adjacent seat. She conjured a vision of Clayton in his passenger traveling pose, chin cradled, feet up on the dash, elbow resting on the open window. So relaxed. So carefree. She hadn't seen him like that since... since forever. He was care*ful* these days. Full of care. So full of care there was no room for anything else. It gutted her seeing him like that, taking on additional weight. He didn't have to do that. He didn't *need* to do that. If only he could share her sense of what was happening, what she was becoming.

Ash plucked the key from her pocket and held it in her closed fist. She squeezed tight, feeling the teeth bite into her palm. It felt good, real. She drew the stem of the key out of her fist, then ran the point down along her exposed thigh. The skin was soft, pliable. Veins glowed in the dim light, like trails of phosphorescence on the night ocean. A ghostly line of tiny half circles started at her knee, wound around her calf and cradled her heel.

She felt nothing.

Ash tapped the key on her chin, inserted it into the ignition and turned it partway. The dashboard dials lit up, chasing the dark into the backseat. The stereo came to life. Paramore's "Misery Business."

Water, she thought. It embraced you, filling all your senses.

"Ash? Are you in here?"

She sighed and pressed the button to open the sunroof.

"I'm here, Dad."

Len Drummond's face appeared at the passenger-side window. "Been looking all over the place. Thought we'd lost you."

"No. Just having some time to myself."

"I'm sorry. I interrupted. Do you want me to come back later?"

"No, it's fine. I'm done."

The elder Drummond held up a hand, then coughed into a handkerchief. "Love, would you mind if we moved outside to the yard? I'd like to talk to you about something."

It was a swim. A long swim. The infamous 180-kilometer stretch between Cuba and the United States. No competitors. No time clock. Just Ash and the water. For what purpose? To set a record, inspire the world. To raise money. A lot of money. And to provide hope. Not just on a global scale—on a personal level too. It would give Ash a goal, a challenge, a process to channel her energies into. It would offer a different opportunity for fulfillment. A chance to become something new.

Ash whistled when her father's pitch was done. "Man, that's quite the sell job. A hundred and eighty kilometers, you say."

"Apparently that is the distance."

She pointed to her legs. "You do realize these aren't the same as before."

"You've been in the pool every day since coming home," said Len, stepping quickly over the statement. "You're strong. Fitter than I've ever seen you. Lord knows it would be hard, but I think you can do it."

"Mum put you up to this, didn't she?"

Len clutched something in his cupped hands. Ash knew he had rosary beads in there. You could almost see the Hail Marys ticking over in his mind.

"Not at all," Len said.

"Not at all?"

"No."

"Not even a little bit?" The clutch intensified. Ash smiled. "You're a terrible liar, Dad. You're going to have to do some extra confession, you know."

"Look, love, the swim…You're keen, aren't you?"

"Why?"

"Why what?"

"Why didn't Mum just come and tell me about this herself? Why did she ask you to do it?"

Len shrugged and stammered. Eventually words formed and tumbled out. "I don't know. Maybe…maybe she just thought it would be better coming from me."

"Because if it came from you there'd be a better chance of me agreeing to it."

"That's not what I meant."

"It's true though. She thinks I'd turn it down just to spite her."

"Would you?" Len sat up a little straighter on the bench. The rotting purple flowers by their feet, courtesy of the nearby jacaranda, lent the air a sickly perfume. "*Thou shall not avenge, nor bear any grudge against the children of thy people, but thou shall love thy neighbor as thyself.*"

Ash sniffed. "My 'neighbor' is the one bearing the grudge, Dad. She can't admit that it's over. Forget Mum for a moment. What do you really think of this? Do you think it's a good idea? You don't, do you? All that shit you were just talking—you don't agree with any of it."

"Don't swear, Ashley. Please."

"Then *you* swear, Dad! Swear to tell the truth for once. You don't want me to have any part of this. Do you?"

"I don't think—"

"Just this one time, tell me you don't want me to do this. *Forbid* me to do it. Go on, say the words. *I forbid you to do this! I am your father, and there is no way in Hell you're going to do this!*"

Len bowed his head and pressed his white-knuckled hands against the bridge of his nose. Veins throbbed in his neck and temples. His heaving chest pumped mutterings of verse from his twitching mouth. It took thirty seconds for a semblance of calm to return. When he dropped his hands to his lap and brought his head back up, Ash was waiting. His daughter's unblinking gaze had not shifted.

"God has a plan," said Len. "Let His will be done."

Ash nodded. "Will be done," she repeated. She shook her head and turned her wheelchair around. On the garden path back toward the house, she spoke over her shoulder.

"I'll do the swim."

Twenty-Five

"Ladies and gentlemen of the media, if I could have your attention, please. Thank you. Thank you very much. Welcome, ladies and gentlemen, to Wake the World, the record swim that will rejuvenate hope, provide inspiration and redefine heroism. Ash was going to start things off by reading a prepared statement, but I believe we've had a slight change of schedule. Is that correct?"

Ash nodded. Blythe hesitated, then nodded too.

"Okay then. Over to you, members of the media. Fire away."

"Wake, when did you decide to do this?"

Ash drank from her sponsor's bottle of sports beverage. Prior to coming onstage, she'd emptied the contents—a cloudy, fizzy, purple liquid—into the bathroom sink and replaced it with tap water.

"Four months, two weeks and five days ago. I came out of physical rehab and I was in the pool, sunup to sundown, working hard. It was like when I was in competition—training, preparing—but it wasn't the same as before the accident. Before the accident, I would be satisfied at the end of a long day in the water. After the accident, I was getting to the end but it wasn't enough. I wanted to keep going. It was my dad who came up with the idea for this. One hundred and eighty kilometers in the ocean. The ultimate swim. He didn't have to do much convincing."

"And now that it's only a few days away, how are you feeling?"

"Not much below the waist." She made a sad trombone noise, disarming the uneasy laughter. "I'm ready."

"How much are you hoping to raise?"

Blythe leaned into the microphones. "Fifty million dollars is the goal for Wake the World. It's ambitious, but we're confident of achieving it. When this is over, Ash Drummond will not only be the first teenage paraplegic to swim the Florida Straits, but she will stand alongside Terry Fox and Rick Hansen as a charity-fundraising icon."

"Ash, this is a grueling swim. You mentioned the distance, but the passage also has the reputation for being treacherous. Susie Maroney felt it was the toughest she ever did. And it has claimed the lives of Cubans trying to get to the States. You are aware of the recent death of Liliana Daminato, who drowned while trying to make the journey in a homemade canoe?"

"I am aware, yes."

"Any concerns for your own safety?"

"Well, we've got a very strong canoe."

More laughter, this time without disquiet.

"But you are doing this swim barely a year after your accident. Do you have any fears your body may give out, may not hold up?"

Blythe, fidgety and breathing hard, started to speak. Ash halted her indignation with an extended arm.

"I'm not worried. I'm built to swim. I always have been. The accident hasn't changed that. I'm at home in the water."

"So you don't think attempting this brutal marathon now is a bit premature?"

"I trust my team. Coach Dwyer knows me better than I know myself. If he says I'm ready, then I know I am. In all honesty, I don't think there could be a better time to do this. Everything has led up to this point. Everything that has happened has been for a purpose."

"Coach Dwyer, this is a pretty remarkable charge you've got here."

"Yes. She is."

"In your mind, how does *first teen paraplegic to swim from Cuba to America*—how does that compare to the Olympic gold that could've been?"

"No comparison."

"You don't think they can be compared, or you don't want to compare them?"

"No comparison."

"Wake—same question."

Ash sat up straighter. "Records and medals are nice, but that was never the motivation for getting in the pool. For me it's all about the moment, the connection. Every time I'm working through my strokes or training, I'm striving to be seamless. To be at one with the water."

"Have you ever achieved perfection?"

"No. But there's still time."

"So you think complete perfection awaits somewhere between Havana and Key West?"

Ash took a sip from her bottle and smiled. "I think so."

⟁

Clayton sat by the fountain, hands burrowed in his jeans pockets. He tried to focus on the warmth of the sunlight, the smell of barbecued onions in the air, the symphony of jets sending streams of water skyward. It was pointless.

The distraction would only last ten seconds or so before his thoughts returned to the post-press conference scene outside the small marquee. Ash, in her chair, barely visible amid the handlers, well-wishers and media.

Her answers, so easy, so straightforward, so likable. And brave. So *very* brave. That was the superficial take, presumably the one that would soon be plastered all over news sites and the evening TV news bulletins. Clayton heard something else in those answers though. Something calculated.

I don't think there could be a better time to do this.

Everything has led up to this point.

Everything that has happened has been for a purpose.

The media knew that purpose. So, too, the viewing audience at home. Ash was a hero. A role model. A beacon of humanity, a symbol of faith. She would make Wake the World a true message of hope and not just another shtick slogan on a colored wristband.

Clayton knew it was a crock. She was covering for something else, something powerful and, in her mind, inevitable. Something she dared not tell.

—◎

Coach Dwyer lobbed a coin into the fountain and patted his comb-over.

"You worried, kid?"

"I'm…confused."

"Did those vultures in there talking about the poor bastard who drowned…did that scare you a bit? Remember, they were on their own. There'll be a dozen people monitoring her. And she'll be in the cage."

"I know the setup. I know she won't be in danger." Clayton shuffled on the spot. "I'd prefer she didn't do this."

Coach Dwyer watched the ongoing post-press-conference scrum. It had thinned in the last few minutes, but catching sight of Ash was impossible. "She's in good nick," he said. "And she wants to do it. Christ knows, I've tried to talk her out of it, but she's made up her mind. She's committed."

Clayton tried to speak, but the words crumbled on his tongue.

"Look," said Coach Dwyer, "I'd rather she didn't do this either. But we don't have a say, do we? This is Ash's decision. And she's made it clear—she's doing it. The only thing we can do is choose whether or not we want to be a part of it." Dwyer placed a hand on Clayton's shoulder. "You can walk away, you know."

"Are you serious?" said Clayton. "I can't walk away now."

Dwyer nodded and sat down at the edge of the fountain. He leaned forward, elbows propped on his knees, hands clasped in front. "You know what, kid? I have a sneaking suspicion this might be it for Ash. She sees this as the last hurrah. She hasn't said anything to me—it's just a hunch. I don't think she wants to be one of these circus acts swimming all these stupid distances, through garbage dumps and oil slicks, wrapped up in the flag of some good cause. It's only a matter of time before she's ready to cut ties with Cyclone Blythe. A short time. Yeah, she might be a changed girl after this is over." He patted Clayton on the shoulder and stood back up. "There might just be a happy ending to this after all."

As the coach shuffled away, a short bald reporter approached him, hoping for one last story-breaking quote. Coach Dwyer waved a hand, told him to get a haircut and a real job, then headed off in the direction of the sausage sizzle laid on by Wake the World's major sponsor.

"Happy ending?" murmured Clayton. "Do those words even go together?"

Twenty-Six

Clayton brought Ash's wheelchair poolside, locked the brakes and draped a towel across the rear handles. Ash vaulted out of the water and pivoted her torso so she was side-on to the chair. She lifted her left leg out, placing it on the long ribbon of drainage grid running parallel to the gutter; she left her right leg dangling in the wash. After a few seconds catching her breath and stretching her neck, she reached up and gripped the armrests.

"You good?" said Clayton.

With a single, effortless movement, Ash hoisted herself onto the cushioned seat of the chair. She turned her head and nodded.

"I'm good."

Clayton released the brake and pulled the chair back from the edge of the pool. Ash placed her palms on the tires, slowing their rotation. "I got it." Clayton continued to assist, forcing Ash to clamp down hard, halting any further movement. "I've got it, Clay."

"You do, don't you."

"What?"

"Forget it."

"No, *what*?"

Ash stopped the chair by the front row of bleachers. Above them, bystanders in the grandstand—athletes, coaches, spectators—pretended not to watch.

"You don't want me to do the swim."

The rising anxiety in Clayton reached the back of his throat. He shook his head.

Ash looked up at the crowd. Heads and bodies turned back to their own business.

"Let's take this somewhere private," she said, nodding toward the change room. Once inside, she couldn't meet his pleading gaze.

"What do you think is going to happen if I do this?" she asked.

"Some sort of transformation is my best guess," Clayton replied, shocked that he'd said the words out loud. "But I think you know."

Ash opened her mouth to respond, then hesitated. What do I know? she thought. Nothing beyond a growing body of evidence, a building sense of method behind the madness. The out-of-body experience during the world-record swim. The accident, the break in her connection to the earth, which appeared now to be some sort of tipping point. The progressive rash of half circles on her legs. Added up, two and two equaled five. That's what she knew. And the assumption had been that only she knew. Not so—her beloved Clayton was doing the same absurd math.

And now the equation was simple: 180 kilometers, twenty-four plus hours. More than enough distance and time for destiny to be satisfied.

"I don't know exactly what's going to happen," she said. "I guess I'll find out."

"You don't have to do it, Ash. You can stay home. Stay with me."

"I'm sorry."

"Don't say that."

"I love you, Clay. Always. But this…I have to do this."

Misery choked the air for a minute or more. Clayton, chest heaving, saw her gesturing for him to come closer. He complied, then fell to his knees on the cold tiled floor. She leaned over the side of the chair and they kissed. As he withdrew, Clayton realized she was crying. He stroked her hair.

"It's like I've been—I don't know—cut loose," she whispered. "Like I'm not attached to the ground anymore. And when I'm in the water…" Ash squeezed her eyes shut.

Tears fell from her jawline like tiny shooting stars. "I'm caught in a rip. You remember how that feels, right? And you remember how to deal with a rip? You don't fight. You don't struggle."

"So that's it? You let this thing overtake you? You give up?"

"No," she said, wiping her cheeks dry. "You let go."

Clayton wrapped his arms around her thin knees and laid his head in her lap. There was a suppleness to her legs now, an elasticity that suggested the bones were shrinking or dissolving. A thin membrane, almost invisible to the naked eye, covered her ankles like gauze. Her toes had lost their nails and were flattening, tapering to points. The marks on her legs gave off a soft glow in the fluorescent light.

Twenty-Seven

On the morning of the first anniversary of the accident, Team Drum milled around the gate, preparing to board the flight to Havana. There was a smattering of interested onlookers. Two journalists. No camera crews. No fans.

Ash scanned the concourse again and again, checking every face among the passengers and well-wishers. She knew she would not see him, but she couldn't stop herself. She imagined him on the escalator to the gate, tablet in hand, lick of coal-black hair falling across his radiant face. She rose from the wheelchair and stood on the legs of a past life. He met her, lifted her up. He cradled her head and dived headlong into her loving gaze.

Take me with you.

"I can't."

You said we'd be together.

"We are."

Always?

"Forever."

Ash went to kiss him, but he wasn't there. He was back on the threshold of the escalator. The steps were now retreating. Clayton mouthed the word *Bye* as his descent began.

"Goodbye, my love."

"Who are you talking to?"

Ash shook her head and spun her chair around.

"Myself, Mum. Getting in the zone. Just like you taught me."

Blythe smiled. She looked at the motley gathering that had come to see them off. Her grin remained, but her tone took on an ominous quality. "Shit turnout. I did cartwheels for them and they can't even be bothered to show. They've written us off, Ash." She prodded her shoulder. "They'll come crawling back when we wake the world."

The smile fell away as Blythe's face settled back into pinched intensity. She lifted the phone from her tracksuit pocket and scrolled through the text messages. She spoke without deviating from the screen.

"What happened to the boy?"

"Clayton."

Blythe shrugged. "Whatever. He sleep in?"

Ash sat up straighter. "We talked yesterday. We broke up."

"Really?"

"Yes."

Blythe feigned a sympathetic "ohhh," then returned to the screen. "It's for the best. For you. And him."

"Mum—"

"At least now you can get rid of that awful ring he gave you. The one on your thumb. What the hell are 'water lovers' anyway?"

Ash leaned forward and slapped the phone out of her mother's grasp, sending it skittering across the floor. Blythe wrung her struck hand, then held it splayed against her chin, a protection against any further attack. Her distended eyes absorbed the changeling before her—the flushed cheeks, the clamped jaw, the right hand set in a fist. The face a line drawn in the sand.

"Don't ever bad-mouth Clayton in my presence again," said Ash, menace fortifying each word. "Got it?"

Limb by limb, muscle by muscle, Blythe shook free of her bewilderment and restored her composure. When at last she stood tall—chin up, battered shoulders back—she retrieved her phone.

"The defining moment of your life is a mere forty-eight hours away, Ashley," she replied. "I suggest you save your energy."

She turned on her heel and strode over to Team Drum, barking out commands that sent minions scurrying in all directions.

Ash pivoted for one last look at the concourse.

Twenty-Eight

Tuula knocked lightly on the closed door to Clayton's room. She entered without waiting for a response. Clayton stared at the tablet, zooming hard into a drawing, obsessing over just the right amount of shading. He would draw, then erase. Draw and erase. Tuula placed a bowl of soup on the desk beside him and sat down on the bed.

"Lapsi? Is this work?"

Clayton didn't respond, didn't acknowledge his grandmother at all.

"I have some kesäkeitto for you. Extra pepper."

"I'm not sick, Mummu."

"You *are* sick. You do not have a fever or the flu or the stomach upset. You have something worse. A sickness of the heart. So eat. It will give your body strength and your heart a small tonic."

Clayton continued with his task. Tuula removed her glasses and balanced them on the alarm clock.

"This is different to the last time. She is not coming back, yes?"

Clayton turned the image ninety degrees and adjusted a line.

"Your eyes are open. I understand what you are seeing. I have seen it myself." She rose from the bed and stood behind him, running her fingers through the hair of the boy she'd held and soothed and shielded from the world more times than she could count.

"I want to tell you a story, lapsi. This is the first time you will be hearing it, because I have never told it to you before. In fact, I have never told it to anyone."

Clayton stopped fussing with the image on screen. He spun around in the chair to face her, and Tuula sat on the end of the bed.

"I was so mad when your isoisä said he was going to Korea a second time. I called him many bad names. Kusipää and *aasi*. He held my face and kissed me and listened to all of my stupidity. He believed I was upset and didn't mean any of the things I said. He was right—I didn't mean what I said. I knew the situation. It was the time of the conscription—he had no choice. If he had refused, he would have been in serious paska. But he wanted to go back. He talked of work left unfinished and friends he had left behind. He reminded me that his *isä* had gone to war. His *isoisä* too. Honor and courage and fighting for the freedom of his country, his people. These were everything to him. I was in his heart, but being a soldier was in his soul. He had to go. And I was afraid.

"When the officer came to the door to tell me he was gone, I did not *itkeä* or scream or any of this. There had been terrible thoughts in my mind all that week and pain in my heart. I had feared the worst, but the officer told me he had disappeared. *Missing in action* were his words. He told me he was sorry and that they were doing everything they could to find him and bring him home. He said other things too, but I stopped listening. I was too busy thinking my own thoughts. Actually, just one: I did not lose you to gunfire or bombs. I lost you to *kohtalo*. To destiny.

"He was never found. He is still missing today. They did everything they could, and then they stopped looking. I wish I had been with him, *lapsi*. Just to see him. To hold his hand. To sing to him, 'I'm Gonna Wash That Man Right Outa My Hair.' To assure him he was a ripper of a hubby, just as Fat Beryl had foretold. To tell him love is the strongest force in all the world! More powerful than the mountains and the skies and the oceans! It is the source of all! To tell him our love will defeat destiny, in this world and the next.

"To cry with him before I cried alone."

Clayton swallowed, and tears welled in his eyes. Tuula smiled sadly. She retrieved her glasses and willed her slightly stooped frame to standing, positioning herself in front of Clayton.

"What?" he said.

"We change places."

Clayton stood and offered the chair to his grandmother. She sat, spun back around to the computer and started irritably stabbing the trackpad. With her other hand, she lit a cigarette.

"What are you doing, Mummu?"

Tuula took a long drag, then stubbed out in the soup. "I am waiting."

"For what?"

"For you to help me with this electronic *elukka*." She extracted a credit card from her pocket. "How to buy an airline ticket to Cuba is a story I cannot tell."

Twenty-Nine

Clayton knew he wouldn't do anything on the plane. The movies would go unwatched. The food and drink cart would pass by without a request. He was more likely to find gold in the seat pocket than conversation with the person sitting beside him. Sleep? Impossible. No matter how tired he was (*tired* was inadequate; some new made-up word was required to describe his exhaustion), there would be no rest on the flight, and certainly none when he reached Havana. Perhaps the capacity to sleep had abandoned him altogether. Clayton didn't dwell. Letting go—the concept had new meaning these days.

He watched the screen on the chair in front. The in-flight stat for kilometers traveled ticked over. Wiping his eyes, he stared at the number, commanding it to speed up.

Thirty

Dressed in shorts and flip-flops, an unshaven Coach Dwyer was waiting at the José Martí International terminal. Much of his comb-over stood at attention. A crumpled sponsor's T-shirt provided flimsy cover for his belly. His frayed appearance matched Clayton's nerves.

"Welcome to Havana, kid," he said. "Pretty sure this place doesn't need waking up."

"Has it started? Has she gone already?"

Dwyer raised a reassuring hand. "Cyclone Blythe's whipping up some wind, but she can't blow out to sea till I'm back. Ash made sure that was clear."

"Does she know I'm here?"

"No. I didn't tell her, like you asked." He scratched the stubble on his chin. "You hopin' for an ambush? Last-ditch bid to talk her out of it?"

Clayton shook his head. "I just want to see her."

"Strangest thing." Dwyer looked around the terminal, taking in the pockets of listless travelers. "*I just want to see him.* Those were the exact words she said to me in Denver." He sucked air through his teeth. "There's not a lot that makes sense in this world, kid, but it makes sense that you're here. I'm pleased you didn't walk away."

Clayton nodded. "Me too."

They moved quickly through the terminal, walking beneath the vast web of pipes and beams in the ceiling, passing under rows of flags from all corners of the globe. Clayton wondered how many people from all those nations were following Ash's attempt at history. How many would reference it in their news? It could be every country on Earth, and Ashley Ray Drummond would still be unknown to them. The truth was so much more than their superficial stories could ever capture, could ever conceive. It was light years beyond anything made for TV or gone viral or dumbed down to one hundred and forty characters. It was timeless, like beauty and memory.

Like love.

⟳

The highway emptied into dimly lit suburban streets, then the city center. The air smelled of dust and tobacco and sweat. Strains of jazz music sauntered through the crack in the driver-side window. Old-world buildings stood side by side, a watchful armada tracking the foreigners' progress. Coach Dwyer, perhaps impelled by their presence, spoke in a conspiratorial tone. "Not long now."

"Okay."

They drove through Chinatown, passed by the Museo Nacional de Bellas Artes de La Habana. Within minutes the water was visible between the luxurious Vedado residences, murky and foreboding, like spilled ink on the canvas of an expensive portrait. It was 4:30 AM.

"We're gonna skip the hotel," said the coach. "Head straight for the charter boat."

"Okay."

"You still got that confused feeling you mentioned back when we spoke?"

Clayton hung a hand out of the open passenger window, catching the wind. "No. I just want to be with her. Whatever happens."

"Well…" Dwyer pointed and pulled the car in to the curb. "*Whatever* is about to happen."

Blythe was waiting.

Thirty-One

"You went to pick up that boy? If I had known that, I would've made sure we got going before you came back."

Coach Dwyer glared as he pushed past her. "I'm sure your daughter feels differently."

"She doesn't," asserted Blythe. "But you got one thing right. *My* daughter. Mine. Flesh and blood. You really think she would take your side? Favor you over her *mother*? You give yourself too much credit."

"Settle down. Hey, kid? She's this way."

"They broke up! And it was never going to work anyway. He didn't belong in her lane."

"Blythe—"

"You've wasted your time and money coming out here, ComicCon. Ash has already moved on. You need to do the same."

Coach Dwyer turned back, but Clayton held a hand up to stop him.

"It's fine, Coach," he said, squaring up to face Blythe. "This ends now."

"You're not going to hit her or anything, are you?"

Clayton laughed. "No, Coach. I'm not."

Blythe looked rough. The light was poor, but not poor enough to hide the cracks in her stony facade. Her hair was bedraggled. Her gait was bowed and stiff. The harrowing glare that was both her weapon and her comfort had lost its authority—it now suggested tiredness and frustration rather than intimidation. Her right eyelid had fluttered throughout the "*my* daughter" tirade.

Dwyer wasn't taking any chances. He circled back and leaned in close to Clayton's ear. "If she comes at you," he muttered, "just keep moving back. Let her wing at you. Those shoulder joints of hers are mush, and all the damage she'll do will be to herself. Understand?"

"Seriously, I'm not going to fight her," Clayton insisted.

"You might not want to, but I don't know about her. She looks madder than a cut snake. I'll be just down the road, where the boat's docked. Any trouble, I'll come running."

"Thanks, Coach."

Dwyer hesitated, then moved away. Before he was out of earshot, he had a parting message for Blythe. "Forget about the world. You should wake up to yourself."

～⊙

Blythe cricked her neck after Coach Dwyer's departure.

"As soon as we touch the beach at Fort Zachary Taylor, he's fired." She pointed to the water of the Canal de Entrada and out into the Atlantic. "So why are you here?"

Clayton held her gaze. "To be here."

"You think she wants to see you?"

"I know she does."

Blythe fell silent, eyes narrowed to slits. She had geared up for domination, for the final extraction of this little thorn in her side. But Clayton's surety had thrown her. He watched the thoughts play out across her reddened face. Confusion, analysis, realization. A firework fizzed somewhere in the Vedado as Blythe brought a hand to her forehead.

"You think you're *coming with us*? You think you'll be *on the boat with us*?"

Clayton crossed his arms. "Yes."

Blythe looked around, pleading with an unseen crowd to back her up.

"I'll tell you what," she said, clapping her hands together. "How about instead of going on the boat you go somewhere else? Why don't you go to hell? Or, better yet, back in time. Yes, go back in time and get in the car alongside Ash when she rolls it in the storm."

Maintaining a sure balance and an even gaze, Clayton took two paces forward, bringing him to within arm's length of her.

"I love Ash," he said. "And that's true whether you choose to accept it or not. I love your daughter. You and I have that in common." He advanced another step and muted his voice. "I feel sorry for you."

"Is that a fact?" said Blythe through clenched teeth.

"Yes."

"Well, well, do share. Why am I so deserving of your precious sympathy?"

"Because you've lost her." Clayton's heart pounded against his chest. "You know that, don't you? You've lost her for good."

Blythe staggered backward before regaining her footing. She glared at Clayton, an invisible fishhook tugging her upper lip. After several seconds the mask of loathing began to shift. Blythe ran her tongue around her teeth and the inside of her cheeks, gathering the available saliva from her rapidly drying mouth. She pursed her lips and jerked her head forward, motioning to spit.

Her target did not flinch. Blythe dropped her head and hawked a coin-sized glob. It touched down centimeters from Clayton's toes.

"Hey!"

Blythe and Clayton turned toward the voice. Ash emerged from under the dimly lit canopy of a nearby cigar store. "Walk away," she said.

Blythe grinned and hiked a thumb over her shoulder. "You heard her, boy."

"I wasn't talking to Clayton, Mum."

"What?"

"I was talking to you. Walk away now. Or there's no swim."

"You don't mean that."

"Try me."

"Ash—"

"I dare you."

A rogue wave pounded the Malecón seawall, sending a primal thump through the pavement and a slingshot of brine toward the last of the night stars. Blythe stiffened, lifted her chin and clawed at her neck, like a dog straining against its leash.

"This is ridiculous," she muttered.

She strode over to her daughter, grasped the armrests of her chair and leaned forward, hoping to touch forehead to forehead. Ash rebuffed the advance by moving back, the sudden movement yanking the armrests from Blythe's grasp and causing her to stumble. Blythe straightened and flicked the hair out of her eyes.

"You don't get to do this," she said, zipping the sponsor's jacket all the way to her throat. "I am your mother! I made you. Everything you were, everything you are, and everything you ever will be is my doing. You understand that?"

Ash nodded. "I do."

"Don't you ever forget it."

Ash shook her head. "I won't."

Blythe gave a satisfied grunt, threw one last kill-shot glare in Clayton's direction and stormed off to prepare for the day she so richly deserved.

Ash crossed the dock to where Clayton still stood. She gestured for him to lean down, then held a hand to the back of his head as she kissed him.

"You couldn't let go," she said once they had released.

"I just want to be here."

"You're shaking."

"Am I?"

"I love you."

"I know."

Ash watched the first sunlight breach the horizon. "Let's go down to the water."

Thirty-Two

The early-morning procession—dog-walkers, joggers, happy-snapping tourists—moved in both directions along the Malecón. Few gave a second glance to the couple in among the coral outcrops—a lovers' embrace was hardly an oddity on the famed seven-kilometer stretch. Those who did look were drawn to the scene by the wheelchair, a rare sight amid the buskers and fishermen and 1950s cars, let alone at the water's edge.

Ash sat on a small flat shelf, legs dangling in the Atlantic. Clayton knelt beside her, then eased into a seated position. Ash slipped her arms around his waist, rested her head on his shoulder. The sunrise nestled at eyeline, orange and bleeding.

"Will you remember me?" asked Clayton.

Ash smiled. "Of course."

"How do you know?"

"Because we're forever."

A puff of spray leaped out of the ocean and fell upon the pair. Ash felt the mist enter her pores. It trickled through her, seeping, soaking in. She drew Clayton close and pressed her damp cheek against his. She touched him, savoring every nuance, casting a net over her memories. Clayton looked down at the water. Ash's feet were fluid, refracting in the shallows.

"Are you scared?" he asked.

Ash buried her face into his shoulder. "Yes," she said, her voice small and strained.

"Don't be," he replied.

Thirty-Three

Later that morning, when Ash entered the shark-proof cage and performed the first of 100,000 strokes that would carry her to the United States, Clayton was below decks. He ignored the excitement of the handlers, their cheers and whistles and the odd "Come on!" as Wake the World got underway. He disregarded the sights swirling past the porthole: the news helicopter in the sky, the honking flotilla chaperoning his beloved's journey to the open sea. When Coach Dwyer sat down beside him and attempted to make conversation, he said he wasn't feeling well.

A half hour after launch, the commotion died away. Clayton closed his eyes and began to draw.

Open.

He exhaled.

Open eyes.

His lids flickered.

Open eyes like Mummu said.

Fighting instinct, Clayton took a peek at his work. It was the familiar landscape. Peace reigned. The ocean was a crystal plain. The colossal wave had withdrawn, leaving the beach alone.

And Ash?

She was gone. A memory. Seamless with the sea. At one with her sacred medium.

Clayton powered down the tablet.

It would remain down for 180 kilometers.

Thirty-Four

At 7:13 AM, approximately 25 hours and 58 minutes after commencement, the Wake the World swim ended at Fort Zachary Taylor Historic State Park in Key West.

The first inkling of concern was felt with the opening of the shark-proof cage. The team member monitoring Ash's vitals reported several data glitches, though these were disregarded as wireless-equipment failures. A disagreement took place between the two "watchers," the people charged with observing Ash from the support vessel's deck. One lost sight of her in the water. The other saw what he would later describe as a "shadow" swimming toward the shore.

Less than a minute after the cage's opening, the small crowd that had gathered on the beach to witness history encountered a sight they would spend a lifetime trying to explain. A junior reporter from the *Miami Herald*, standing at the edge of the group, was the first to notice.

He dropped his phone, shouting like a banshee, and pointed a shaking finger at the shallows. All eyes fell upon the impossible spectacle in his crosshairs.

A translucent female form, seemingly conjured from the blue-green depths of the Gulf Stream, crested a wave that carried her out of the surf and onto the sand. Surrounded by tufts of foam and strips of kelp, she paused for a moment, head bowed. Then she lifted herself out of the wash. Some of her liquid form was human in shape. Bare, broad shoulders. Whorls of dark hair. Long, serpentine arms. Her heaving torso was lean, the sculpted abdominal muscles rolling like a set of breakers. Other features entered the domain of pure imagination. Sprouting from her upper back were wings, aqueous folds more delicate than a spider's web. Swathed over her obscured legs was a gossamer-thin wrap, dotted with pale blue half circles.

The morning sun refracted through her. The horizon, though distorted, was framed by her rib cage. She extended an arm, reaching tentatively toward land.

Fear and confusion gripped the crowd. Some turned to Team Drum for answers. They had none.

Len looked skyward, reciting his words of refuge: "…forgive us our trespasses, as we forgive those who trespass against us, and lead us not into temptation, but deliver us from evil…" Prayer would be lost to him after that day.

Coach Dwyer watched in stone-faced silence. The vision of Fort Zachary Taylor would haunt him until his dying day. He never spoke of it though. Not even to the hundreds of swimmers he coached in the Paralympics and Invictus Games.

Blythe stood, eyes wide, mouth gaping, fingers poking at her shoulders, pained squeaks eking out of her throat. Over the next ten years, she would scour every fathom of the Gulf Stream for her lost girl. The ten following she would unsuccessfully sue everyone and everything connected to Wake the World. Her last five would be in the care of a mental-health facility.

Among the shell-shocked group, Clayton was the only one to move. He ran to the water's edge. Heart flailing in his chest, he dropped to his knees and threw his arms around her. She was rapidly losing form. The wave carrying her had withdrawn, exposing her to the light and to the air. He pulled close, shut his eyes and kissed her. Tears were swamped in the deluge. Water was on his tongue, in his throat. Entering him. Filling him. Washing away flesh and bone. He opened his eyes. For a fleeting moment he was the ocean. An infinite blue.

Then she was gone, melted, sliding back into the sea.

Several cameras—video and still—attempted to capture the moment. They failed. Ashley Ray Drummond was elusive to the lens, a wrinkle that could easily be dismissed as shadow or digital artifact.

Clayton wiped his face, his eyes. His arms throbbed, crying out for a connection lost. He bowed his head. Nestling against his right knee was a dash of silver. He plucked the object from the sand and held it to his lips. The water-lover ring.

He knew Ash was home now.

Knew it as true love knows eternity.

Thirty-Five

Clayton opened the front door of his townhouse and drifted over the threshold. A newspaper wrapped in plastic lay beside the *tervetuloa* mat. On the breakfast bar, a bunch of white roses craned from a crystal vase filled almost to the brim with water. In the living room, the TV prattled. Clayton shrugged the bag off his shoulder as familiar aromas from the kitchen teased his red, blotchy nose. Onions and peas, milk and pepper. Kesäkeitto.

He found Tuula standing in the hallway, her eyes glistening. She shared no words—just a look that cradled his aching heart. After several seconds she opened her arms, and he fell into them. Her tears were cool on his cheek. He was grateful for them.

Like wounded soldiers, they leaned against each other, shuffling down the hallway. The TV grew louder at the end of the passage. The news was on.

"*…The whereabouts of swimming champion Ashley Drummond remains a mystery seventy-two hours after her dramatic disappearance at Key West in Florida. An extensive search-and-rescue operation has found no trace of the former world-record holder, leading to theories that she may have been attacked by a shark close to shore. Local authorities are still reaching out to eyewitnesses to try and provide some clue as to what happened—firsthand accounts to this point have been, according to police chief Pedro Mosqueda, 'unusual and erratic'…*"

"Ay, lapsi," said Tuula. "Stay here."

She patted Clayton's hand and, with a spryness not ordinarily associated with seventy-three-year-old, chain-smoking grandmothers, scampered into the living area to snatch up the remote control from the coffee table. She stabbed button after button, then hurled the remote at the nearby bookshelf. The screen went blank.

"Agh," she said. "That show is shit. Not the shit. Just shit. You okay?"

"I'm good," replied Clayton.

"Yes?"

"Yes."

"Good."

"Actually," added Clayton, "I have a story like that one on the TV. Have I told it to you before, Mummu?"

"Ay, you have."

"How many times?"

"Heaps."

"How many?"

Tuula closed one eye and counted the nicotine-stained fingers on her right hand. "One hundred and twenty-seven times."

Clayton nodded. "Not enough."

Tuula laughed. "Come," she said, taking hold of his elbow. "Tell me after you rest."

Inside his room, Clayton sat down on the bed. Tuula asked if he would like to cover up—he declined.

"I need to check on the soup," she said. "But I will be back minuutissa." She squeezed his shoulder and retreated. At the door she paused. "I like the beautiful new ring on your thumb, lapsi."

Tuula exited, quietly singing a tune: "*I'm gonna wash that man right out of my hair…I'm gonna wash that man right out of my hair…*"

⌒◡

Prior to sleep Clayton opened his tablet and drew. No semiconsciousness needed for this piece, no whimsical artistry required. It was focused, intended.

The canvas was layered in rich watercolor textures of deep blue and green, the hues of a forbidding wave caught at its peak. The figure in the center was little more than a delicate outline. Her back was turned and she faced outward, directly into the blue. She wore a racing swimsuit cut low on her back. Arms extended. Feet apart and planted. Her hair flowed like faint, thin tentacles, more ocean than human. She was translucent, at one with the water.

More subtle, though, was the second presence—a boy, looking on from a rocky outcrop in the distance, barely there. One hand on his heart. The other waving goodbye.

The image had a title, applied by the app, though there'd been a glitch in its standard numbering system. The filename read *Source__*.

Clayton smiled. It wasn't something missing, that tiny open space. It was a presence, constant and connected.

A marker of infinite possibility.